Dear Reader:

Welcome to my world of L.A. CONNECTIONS. I have been toying with the idea for some time of writing a serial novel, and last year when I wrote a special four-part series for *TV Guide,* and received so many of your wonderful letters, I knew that I wanted to make it bigger and better! L.A. CONNECTIONS is a story about a high-profile murder in Los Angeles. This four-part novel brings together a group of diverse characters—true-life people, cleverly disguised, that I have observed in all the years I have lived in Hollywood.

I know many of you loved the character of Lucky Santangelo, a heroine I created in four of my books: *Chances, Lucky, Lady Boss,* and *Vendetta: Lucky's Revenge.* In L.A. CONNECTIONS, I have tried to create characters just as charismatic.

Writing is my passion, and bringing a serial novel to life is a wonderful challenge. First comes *Power,* followed by *Obsession,* then *Murder,* and finally, *Revenge.*

When you read something that really grabs your attention, it should be a great visual trip so that you can imagine the characters. In all my seventeen books, I feel I've captured the essence of the lives I have observed. Of course, I've changed the names to protect the not-so-innocent!

Writing L.A. CONNECTIONS was an adventure. I hope you join me for all four parts, and that it will keep you reading way into the night.

Stay with me—I promise you we'll have fun!

Happy Reading,

Meet the Men and Women Caught Up in the Shattering Secrets of *REVENGE*

Madison Castelli: The feisty, smart, sensual journalist is sent to L.A. to interview Hollywood superagent Freddie Leon for the magazine *Manhattan Style*. Instead she's swept into the biggest crime story of the year, and into a desire that may shatter her tough professionalism or her heart.

Kristin Carr: More Norma Jean than Marilyn, her wholesome, nubile looks are a titillating contrast with her talents—as a high-priced call girl, specializing in rich and famous clients. Risk is all part of her job, and so is servicing Max Steele *and* Mister X.

Freddie Leon: A driven, devious deal-maker who manipulates his celebrity clients like a puppet master, he has enormous power, a hidden agenda, and a star's erotic eight-by-ten glossies locked up in his safe . . . for insurance.

Max Steele: Still boyish looking at 42, in shape, and happiest behind the wheel of a shiny red Maserati or luring a lady into his bedroom, he's Freddie Leon's longtime partner . . . and the worst mistake he could make would be to become his enemy.

Jake Sica: Easy charm, laughing eyes, and sexual heat on sizzle, this freelance photographer holds a natural attraction for any SWF . . . but he has fallen hard, fast, and furiously for a blond beauty whose secrets mask a deadly double life.

Natalie De Barge: Like a five-foot-two case of dynamite, this black and beautiful, vivacious newscaster just needs some heat to ignite an explosive career. Now with her best friend Madison visiting, she's about to be cast into the fire of a breaking story.

Cole De Barge: Natalie's handsome, gay brother—a fitness trainer who *really* knows the secrets of the stars.

Mister X: The identity of the man who likes his sex strange, kinky, and dangerous is as hidden as his dark soul. His obsession is to experience ecstasy beyond the limits, where fear and death meet. . . .

Books by Jackie Collins

Revenge
Murder
Obsession
Power
Thrill!
Vendetta: Lucky's Revenge
Hollywood Kids
American Star
Lady Boss
Rock Star
Hollywood Husbands
Lucky
Hollywood Wives
Chances
Lovers and Gamblers
The World Is Full of Divorced Women
The Love Killers
Sinners
The Bitch
The Stud
The World Is Full of Married Men

JACKIE COLLINS

Revenge

POCKET BOOKS

New York London Toronto Sydney Tokyo Singapore

This book is a work of fiction. Names, characters, places and incidents are products of the author's imagination or are used fictitiously. Any resemblance to actual events or locales or persons, living or dead, is entirely coincidental.

An *Original* Publication of POCKET BOOKS

POCKET BOOKS, a division of Simon & Schuster Inc.
1230 Avenue of the Americas, New York, NY 10020

Copyright © 1998 by Chances, Inc.

ISBN: 0-671-02461-2

First Pocket Books printing December 1998

10 9 8 7 6 5 4 3 2 1

POCKET and colophon are registered trademarks of Simon & Schuster Inc.

Back cover photo by Greg Gorman

Printed in the U.S.A.

chapter 1

THE GIRL WAS BARELY MORE than sixteen. The pupils of her large hazel eyes were enormous. So was her sexual appetite.

Bobby Skorch had picked her up on Sunset as soon as he'd been able to get out of the house, which had been a hassle due to all the fuss over his wife—superstar sex symbol Salli T. Turner—who had gotten herself murdered the night before.

That Salli, Bobby thought, his mind mired in a drugged-out haze, *you never knew what she was going to do next, always full of surprises.*

Finally he'd managed to sneak out of the house by lying on the floor in the back of his maid's car. She'd dropped him off at a hotel where he kept a permanent penthouse suite in his manager's name.

Later he'd taken a cruise along Sunset in the black

Ferrari he kept in the basement parking area of the hotel—also registered in his manager's name.

The girl had been hanging around outside a club, and she'd willingly accompanied him back to his hotel. Now she was riding his dick like she was competing in some kind of equestrian event. He didn't have to do a thing except lie back and tolerate the ride, because he certainly wasn't enjoying it. This girl wasn't Salli. *Nobody* was Salli. She was one of a kind. The others were all slags and sluts and whores.

He had no idea what the girl's name was, or whether she had AIDS or the clap—he didn't care.

Bobby was into taking risks. He'd taken a big risk marrying Salli, whom many people had considered a joke with her large fake tits and cascades of dyed platinum hair.

But hey, a lot of *her* friends had considered *him* a risk. Bobby Skorch, the original danger man, with tattoos from here to Cuba, including one on his famous dick.

All he knew was that together they were an awesome sight. *S'long, Pammy and Tommy, Heather and Richie. The Skorches ruled.*

And he'd loved her with a burning passion. Now she was gone.

The girl spread her legs even wider, practically balancing her mothlike weight on his dick. Then she moaned—a prelude to ecstasy.

He wasn't there. Not even close. He was hard and angry and stoned and in the worst pain of his life.

When the girl's moans turned to orgasmic cries and he felt her coming, he screamed his anguish so loud that two maids working on the penthouse floor came running to hover outside the door of Suite 206, their eyes bulging with fear and curiosity.

Satisfied and more than a tiny bit alarmed, the young girl rolled off him, quickly scurrying to get into her clothes. When she reached the door, she looked back at the man, still spread-eagled on the bed, still erect.

There *was* no release for Bobby Skorch. He was in hell.

And there was absolutely nothing he could do about it.

chapter 2

"T HE GUY HAS PUSSY FOR breakfast," Detective Lee Eccles said, chewing on a ragged toothpick.

"What?" said Detective Tucci, distracted as he pored over his copious notes on the Salli T. Turner murder.

"Salli's old man, Bobby Skorch. His cock is bigger than the Empire State Building—an' every broad in Vegas has had herself a slice."

Tucci removed his glasses, glanced up at his partner—whom he didn't particularly like—and nodded. "I know. He has quite a reputation."

Tucci's wife, Faye, had informed him last night—when he'd gotten home after midnight—that Bobby Skorch was the king of the tabloids. "Not that I read those rags," she'd quickly assured him. "Only some-

4

times I can't help it when I'm waiting in the checkout line at the market."

Sure, Faye, he'd thought affectionately. *Why don't you admit that it's your secret vice? You're like a teenage boy hiding his* Playboy *magazines.*

But then he had his secret vices too, food being one of them. Especially since Faye had put him on a rigid diet. No fats. No sugars. Life was hardly worth living.

He'd already checked out Bobby Skorch. It turned out that Salli's husband had quite a rap sheet. Two arrests for drunken driving; assault with a deadly weapon—the weapon being a broken vodka bottle with which he'd made an unprovoked attack on a photographer; unlawful possession of a firearm; driving with a suspended license; and sexual battery of a teenage girl. The usual celebrity list of misdemeanors.

Tucci sighed and looked up at Lee, who was now perched on the edge of his desk, cleaning his dirty fingernails with the wooden toothpick. "What else did you find out in Vegas?" he asked.

"Plenty," Lee said, digging deep. "Saturday afternoon our boy performed a motorcycle stunt, jumpin' over like a hundred and three cars—some kind of crazy shit. Came out of it without a scratch. After that, he took himself to a lap-dancin' joint, where he picked up three strippers an' ferried 'em back to his hotel. Then I guess he partied for a coupla hours, an' when he finally left, the doorman told me he still had two of the girls with him."

"You mean he brought them back to L.A.?" Tucci asked, considering the possibilities.

"They were in his limo when he left the hotel." Lee

paused for dramatic effect. "But here's the kicker. Bobby didn't *drive* back to L.A. like Marty Steiner said. He took a private plane. So *why* is his asshole lawyer tellin' us he was in the car for five hours? The fucker *flew* back. I already questioned the pilot—he told me they arrived in L.A. at eight—which just *might* have given him time to get to the house, kill his wife, an' who knows what else."

"The strippers were on the plane?"

"Yeah."

"Who met them at the airport?"

"A limo. I'm tryin' to locate the driver. The jerk's taken off on vacation. Limo company's trackin' him for me."

"And the strippers?"

"I'm on it."

I bet you are, Tucci thought. When it came to women, Lee was a disrespectful dog, given to making sexist and derogatory remarks. It was one of the reasons Tucci couldn't stand him. That and the fact that Lee had once had a date with Tucci's wife—long before they'd met—but it still bothered him, especially since Faye refused to discuss it.

He'd already decided that as soon as this case was put to bed he was requesting a new partner.

"Any action on the lab reports?" Lee asked.

"She had consensual sex shortly before her death. Put up quite a struggle when the stabbing frenzy began. The lab is analyzing the skin under her finger-nails and fibers found on her body. There's also blood that isn't hers."

Lee nodded, hitched himself off Tucci's desk and strolled over to the coffee machine. Tucci watched him go. All day long he'd had a weird feeling. He'd investigated twenty-six murders and this one was giving him the most trouble. He couldn't help picturing Salli's hacked-up body, lying in a pool of blood. Salli T. Turner. So young and vibrant and pretty. So horribly butchered.

Salli T. Turner was headline news, and not just in the tabloids. Her image was everywhere. The blonde of the day. Little Miss Murdered TV Sex Symbol. The girl in the black rubber swimsuit. Star of the hit TV show *Teach!* and a hundred magazine covers.

Who'd killed her in such a vicious and unconscionable way? he wondered. The public wanted answers. So did Tucci's captain—not to mention the mayor. And Tucci wouldn't mind knowing himself.

The two chief suspects were her current husband, Bobby Skorch, and her recent ex, Eddie Stoner. Both men had a proclivity toward violent behavior—especially concerning women.

Eddie had his own rap sheet—which included getting busted for possession of cocaine, assaulting a police officer, and several domestic abuse arrests. Salli had certainly picked herself a couple of charmers.

Tucci bent over his desk, concentrating on his closely written notes. He had always found that when investigating a murder, it was of major importance to write even the smallest thing down while the evidence was still fresh. Not that he had much evidence to work with: No fingerprints. No witnesses. No murder weapon.

Where was he supposed to start? Ah yes, the bullet extracted from the wall near Froo the houseman's residence. The unfortunate man had been in the wrong place at the wrong time. Probably alarmed by the loud music and the frantic barking of Salli's two small dogs, he'd gone to investigate. Maybe he'd even heard her screams, although none of the neighbors had mentioned hearing screaming—only the music and the dogs. Of course, in Salli's neighborhood the houses were so goddamn big he was surprised they'd heard anything at all. The bullet that had obliterated Froo's face had embedded itself in the wall. Tucci was checking on any guns registered to Bobby or Eddie.

He'd already decided to interview the neighbors again. Sometimes a twenty-four-hour break would give people time to remember things they hadn't considered important.

Details—that's what solving a murder case was all about. Details.

Detective Tucci was known for his detail work.

8

chapter 3

THE OFFICE BUILDING THAT
housed I.A.A. was impressive. Designed by the premier modern architect, Richard Meier, the man who
was also responsible for the splendid new Getty
Museum, the clean lines were superb. Acres of Italian
marble and pristine white walls with just the right
amount of glass block. Dominating everything was a
huge David Hockney painting of a swimming pool
hanging in the massive lobby.

Madison Castelli took all this in as she approached
the front desk. "I'm here to see Mr. Leon," she
announced.

The Asian woman at the reception desk glanced up.
"Do you have an appointment?"

"I certainly do," Madison replied.

"Please take a seat," the woman said.

Instead of going straight to the seating area, Madison strolled across the lobby and stood under the Hockney painting, gazing up at the impressive work of art. As a journalist she loved observing visual images. Capture those and you had your reader hooked. She found Hockney's work to be arresting and very Californian—which was interesting considering he was from England.

Well, here I am in the lobby of I.A.A., she thought, her mind working overtime. She glanced at her watch, noting that it was exactly eleven o'clock, the time of her appointment. She wondered how much time Freddie would grant her, and if he was as intimidating as his reputation.

Freddie Leon was known as the most important agent in town. He was also known as the most reclusive, and it had been tough arranging this interview. Finally, her editor, Victor Simons, had called in a favor, and now here she was. She was intrigued at the prospect of meeting him, but also anxious to get on with it. She wanted to get out of there in time to attend Salli T. Turner's funeral this afternoon.

Ever since her arrival in L.A. three days ago, so much had taken place. On the plane flying out she'd sat next to Salli T. Turner. They'd started talking, arranged an interview, and on the day of the shocking murder she'd lunched with Salli at her house. That night, while dining with friends, she'd heard the unbelievable news of Salli's murder.

This wasn't the way she'd planned her trip, but if she'd learned one lesson in life, it was that there was always something around the corner to surprise you.

Such as her live-in love of two years, David, running out for a pack of cigarettes one day and failing to return. Actually, she didn't much care anymore. In a way she was glad David had gone. Maybe she'd loved him for a while; now he was becoming a distant memory.

Last night, at the insistence of her old college friend, Natalie, with whom she was staying in L.A., she'd gone out on a date with Jake Sica, who happened to be the brother of Jimmy Sica—the anchorman at the TV station where Natalie worked as the show-biz reporter. Jake was interesting and attractive, and they'd had a good time together. But halfway through the evening he'd confessed that he was involved with someone else.

"Why aren't you with her?" she'd asked, concealing her disappointment, because she'd thought he might have been a contender.

"Well . . ." he'd said, and then proceeded to tell her the story of Kristin, who, to his shock, he'd found out was a highly paid call girl.

Wow! Madison had thought. *Well at least we have something in common—bad judgment!*

She'd decided that if Jake ever got over Kristin, maybe they'd get together again, because he was a genuinely nice guy—unlike his brother, Jimmy, who appeared to be a major lech.

She glanced over at the reception desk. The Asian woman was busy on the phone. Hmm . . . It was her experience that the more important the subject, the less they kept you waiting. She made a mental bet that Freddie would summon her to his office within five minutes, and she was right. "Miss Castelli," the woman called out less than two minutes later. "Somebody's on their way down to fetch you."

"Thanks," Madison said.

Moments later a young black man in a spiffy suit and expensive horn-rimmed glasses appeared at her side. "Miss Castelli?" he asked politely.

"That's right," she said.

"Please come with me."

She followed him to a glass enclosed elevator. They traveled up three floors, then walked down a long corridor flanked with many open door offices. Finally they reached the desk of Ria Santiago, Freddie Leon's executive assistant and sentinel.

"Good morning, Miss Castelli," Ria said. She was an attractive Hispanic woman in her mid-forties with a stern expression.

"Good morning, Ms. Santiago," Madison responded. "I'm sorry I disturbed you by calling you at home yesterday. I was under the impression that everyone knew about my visit here."

"Apparently they do now," Ria said, with a thin smile. "Mr. Leon's expecting you. Please come with me."

Madison followed her into a spacious office with an incredible view of Century City. The room was decorated more like a library than a working office; there were large couches on either side and expensive art on the walls. In the middle of the room was the great Freddie Leon, seated behind a magnificent steel and glass desk, poring over papers. He did not look up when she entered.

"Take a seat," Ria Santiago said, indicating a Biedermeier chair to the side of his desk.

Madison had a feeling that if she didn't exert herself immediately she would be hustled out within fifteen minutes.

"Mr. Leon," Ria said, all business. "Your eleven-thirty called to say they'll be five minutes late. I'll alert you three minutes before they're due."

Hmm . . . Madison thought. *Does he really think I'll be satisfied with half an hour? No way.*

Ria left the office. Freddie continued to study the papers on his desk.

"Good morning, Mr. Leon," Madison said, determined to make her presence felt. "I'm delighted you agreed to see me."

Freddie put down his pen and looked up at her for the first time. He saw a beautiful, slender woman in her twenties, with jet hair pulled back, large eyes and full lips.

She stared right back at him, taking in *his* appearance. She saw a poker-faced man in his forties, with cordial features, straight brown hair and a quick bland smile, which she noticed was not reflected in his eyes.

"Good morning, Miss Castelli," he said. "As I'm sure you've been told, I'm seeing you as a favor. I don't normally give interviews."

"I understand, Mr. Leon. I've sat down with a lot of people who don't normally give interviews. Sometimes my subjects find it an enjoyable experience, sometimes they hate it." She smiled. "Let's hope you find it enjoyable."

He smiled back—once again the smile not quite

reaching his eyes. "I'm really extremely boring and very dull," he said, tapping his index finger on his chin.

"Isn't that for *me* to say?" she said, slightly amused.

"It depends. What kind of a journalist are you?"

"Maybe you should ask some of my other subjects," she answered calmly. "Henry Kissinger, Fidel Castro, Margaret Thatcher, Sean Connery. Take your pick."

"Quite an eclectic group," he said. "I'm duly impressed."

"Perhaps you wouldn't be if you read the pieces."

"I'd like to read them."

"Then I'll make sure they're faxed to you this afternoon."

He was summing her up, trying to decide what he thought of her. "Now," he said, "before you start bombarding me with questions, I should tell you that I do *not* discuss the money my clients make. In fact, I do *not* discuss my clients period. I don't talk about my family, politics, sex, or my personal opinions on anything."

Madison laughed politely. "Wow! This is going to be some story!"

He liked the fact that she didn't seem to be in awe of him; it made for a refreshing change. "You don't seem to understand, Miss Castelli—I do not *want* to *be* a story in your magazine."

"Mr. Leon," she said patiently. "There's a great amount of public interest in what goes on in Hollywood, and you are the absolute power broker. People have heard about you, you have a famous name. Sometimes, when we achieve greatness in our lives, we have to give up our privacy."

"I don't have to give up anything, Miss Castelli."

"I wish you'd call me Madison."

There was something in her eyes that drew him in. She was not the normal pushy journalist he was used to encountering at openings and parties. This was an intelligent woman who knew what she wanted and had no fear of pursuing it. For a moment he forgot she was the enemy. "Can I offer you a drink? Apple juice, Diet Coke . . ."

"How about I buy *you* a coffee, somewhere other than your office."

He raised his eyebrows. "Excuse me?"

"Oh, please," she said lightly, playing with him. "I know the game. Your eleven-thirty is running five minutes late—I don't think so. Why don't we get out of here, drive somewhere, grab a coffee and talk about how you got into this business? People would kill to know how you got started."

"Now let's not get dramatic."

"I promise I won't pry into your personal life. I merely wish to portray you as an ordinary human being who has achieved great power, not as some ice-cold Hollywood mogul—which is the impression everyone has of you."

He couldn't help laughing, which he found to be a relief after the stress of the last twenty-four hours. "You're very persuasive . . . Madison. To tell the truth, I wouldn't mind getting out of here, it's been one of those mornings."

"*Can* I buy you a coffee then?" she asked, fixing him with a strong gaze.

She was a beautiful, smart woman, and smartness had always intrigued him. "Why not?" he said, surprising himself. "I suppose I can live dangerously for once."

He got up from behind his desk, and together they walked out of his office.

Ria gave him a stony stare. "Mr. Leon," she said, her voice full of disapproval. "What about your eleven-thirty?"

"Postpone it," he said easily. "I'll be back in an hour. Miss Castelli has persuaded me to play hooky."

Ria frowned. It was unlike Freddie Leon to be so lighthearted. "Very well," she said, tight-lipped. "If you're absolutely sure."

"Yes, I'm sure, Ria."

"And if the hospital calls—"

"You have my numbers."

chapter 4

KRISTIN COULDN'T STOP shivering. She was naked and alone, locked in some funky little beach house where she'd been held captive all night.

She was not afraid. She refused to be afraid. This was another one of Mister X's sick sex games, and now that it was light outside, she was confident he would soon come back to release her.

Last night she'd met him at the end of the Santa Monica Pier, as arranged. As usual he was dressed as a chauffeur—all in black with a baseball cap pulled down low over his forehead, and oblique wraparound shades hiding his eyes.

"Where are we going?" she asked, as he gripped her arm and led her back to his car—a limo.

"You'll know when we get there," he said.

Mister X was a man of mystery, and for her sins she was getting used to his odd ways.

Kristin had climbed into the back of the limo, thinking that however bad her life was, at least she was luckier than her sister, Cherie, who was lying in a coma in a private nursing home because she'd chosen the wrong guy to get engaged to. Howie Powers—a no-good playboy with too much of his daddy's money.

"Put on the blindfold," Mister X commanded.

She'd done as he asked, covering her eyes with the soft velvet mask that was lying on the backseat. As she did it, she told herself, *I'm a paid whore, I deserve everything I get.*

Mister X had then driven along the Pacific Coast Highway at great speed for about twenty minutes, turning off at what felt like a bumpy dirt road. When the car had finally come to a halt he'd thrown open the rear door and almost dragged her out.

She could hear the roar of the sea and smell the cold night air, and for a moment she'd felt fear. "Can I take off the blindfold?"

"No," he replied, roughly gripping her arm and proceeding to take her on a trip down perilous steps to what she assumed was a house. Several times she nearly fell, but he yanked her up. Finally they entered the house, which smelled musty and damp. He led her to a bed, pushed her onto it and said, "Strip."

"What?"

"You heard me."

This was her worst experience with him yet. The man was a true pervert—getting his kicks from frightening people.

"First I want my money," she said, berating herself for not asking earlier.

"Spoken like a true whore," he said, shoving an envelope stuffed with cash at her. She felt the stack of bills with her hands and was instantly reassured. This much money would pay her sister's nursing home bills for months.

"Strip," he repeated in a flat monotone. "Slowly."

She stood up and did as he asked. Hating him. Hating herself.

Standing there naked, she felt vulnerable and exposed. This man who had asked her to do a variety of perverted deeds had never once touched her sexually. Was he finally going to make love to her?

Suddenly she heard the door slam, followed by the click of a heavy lock. Next she heard wild laughter from outside. Then silence.

She waited a few minutes before ripping off the blindfold. The room was pitch black—she couldn't see a thing, there was no light coming in at all.

It was then she realized she was totally alone.

She didn't panic. This was only another way Mister X had of getting his sick kicks.

After a while she began groping around for her clothes, only to discover the perverted freak had taken them.

She edged her way slowly around the small room, feeling ahead of her with her hands. First she tried the door; it was firmly locked. Next to it was a window, which on examination appeared to be boarded up. No getting out of there until he chose to come back, so she settled on the narrow bed, covered herself with the one thin sheet and attempted to sleep.

Now it was morning, light was creeping through the small gaps in the sturdy boards covering the window, and soon Mister X would be back to release her.

No matter how much money he offered in the future, this encounter was definitely the final one. She would *never* do business with him again.

chapter 5

ANGELA MUSCONNI, HOT young actress, knew she was doing the wrong thing, but then Angie had not gotten where she was today by doing the right thing. So against her better judgment, she bailed out her old boyfriend, Eddie Stoner, who might or might not be a suspect in the violent murder of his ex-wife, Salli T. Turner.

Eddie had gotten himself arrested for unpaid parking tickets and his lawyer had vanished on him—so he'd called Angie and asked *her* to put up his bail. She threw down the appropriate money, and had him out of there in no time.

Eddie was delighted to see her, and so he *should* be. It had been three years since he'd left her, and in those three years she'd become a bankable movie star.

Obviously Angie still harbored feelings for Eddie—even though she lived with Kevin Page, another hot

21

young movie star—otherwise she never would have agreed to bail him out.

"You look amazin', Angelina," Eddie said, seated in her Ferrari as she drove him to his apartment.

"I *should* look great," she boasted, thinking that he didn't look as hot as she remembered. "Like I'm a big movie star now."

"Glad it happened for one of us," he said, scratching his stubbled chin.

"It could still happen for you," she said, driving recklessly. "You're not too old. What are you—twenty-nine?"

"Thirty," he said grimly. "Thirty and fucked."

"Can't be all bad," she said lightly.

"Get *this* shit," he said, outraged. "Those filthy pigs dragged me out of bed in the middle of the night an' threw me in jail. They freakin' think *I* did it."

"Did what?" she asked innocently.

"Killed Salli."

"Did you?" she asked, throwing him a sly sideways glance.

"No freakin' way," he said vehemently. "How could you even *think* I'd do somethin' like that?"

"You used to beat the shit out of us, Eddie," she reminded him. "Me *and* Salli. You can't deny it."

"So once in a while I got a little carried away," he said with a careless shrug.

Angie remembered him getting more than a little carried away. Eddie in a rage with his eyes bulging was not a pretty sight. Before Salli had stolen him from her, he'd been a violent bastard, prone to beating her up whenever he felt like it.

"Did you get carried away with Salli on Saturday

night?" she asked boldly, secure that now she was famous he wouldn't dare touch her.

"What're *you?*" he said, scowling. "A freakin' cop?"

"Just askin'. No need to go nuts."

"I'm gonna tell you who did it," Eddie said, nodding his head. "Her moron husband, Bobby, *that's* who."

"How do *you* know?" Angie questioned. "It was probably some crazy stalker. I've got a ton of 'em. I'm sure Salli did, too."

"It was Bobby," Eddie repeated. "He's a stoned psycho—I've seen him in action."

"Doing what?"

"Anythin' he can," Eddie said ominously. "Drive faster," he added. "I wanna get to the TV, see what's goin' on. The cops told me she was hacked to death. What else are they sayin'?"

"Not a lot."

When they reached his apartment one thing led to another, and before she knew it, Angie found herself back in his bed. Sex with Eddie was everything she remembered—and more. Eddie might not be a star on the screen, but he was certainly an above-the-line performer between the sheets. A sexual box-office hit.

When they were finished, she knew she should dress and go home to Kevin—who was in bed waiting for her, expecting her to bring food. But Eddie was back in her life, and Eddie was her addiction—an addiction she'd thought she was over. Apparently not.

"Why'd you dump me and marry Salli?" she asked, leaning on one elbow and staring at him accusingly as they lay in bed. "I was only a baby. *You* treated me like I was nothin'."

"You're *still* a baby," Eddie said, grinning, because he was well aware he was the greatest cocksman that ever lived. Women were so damn easy, give 'em head for ten minutes and they were his forever. "An' rich, too, I bet."

"You got *that* right," she said, giggling.

"What're you doin' with all your loot?" he asked, reaching for a cigarette on the bedside table.

"Whatever I want," she answered cheekily.

"You goin' with anybody?" he asked, keeping his tone deliberately casual.

"Don't you read the fan magazines?"

"Oh, yeah," he said sarcastically. "Like I'm freakin' *glued* to the fan magazines."

"I'm living with Kevin Page."

"Kevin Page?" he snorted. *"That* fairy."

"He's not a fairy," she said defensively.

"Get a life, sweetheart," Eddie said, blowing smoke in her face. "He's gay as a two-cent piece."

"Kevin is *not* gay."

"Yeah?" he said, tweaking her left breast. "I bet he doesn't do it to you like I do."

This was true. Kevin might be on the cover of every teenage girl's fan magazine, but as a lover, he had a lot to learn. "You're *sooo* conceited," she said with a sigh, longing for his hands all over her, not to mention his tongue where it would do her the most good.

Eddie laughed confidently. "So what else is new?"

chapter 6

"WHAT WAS THAT ABOUT a hospital?" Madison asked, as she settled next to Freddie Leon in the passenger seat of his gleaming maroon Rolls-Royce.

"Off the record?" he said briskly.

"Of course."

"My partner was shot last night."

"Max Steele?"

"You know him?"

"Yes, we went jogging together a couple of days ago."

"You get around."

"Is he okay?"

"It hasn't hit the news yet," Freddie said, gazing straight ahead as he drove along Santa Monica Boulevard. "Right now he's in intensive care. My wife is sitting vigil at his bedside."

"This is terrible news."

"It's the reason I agreed to get out of the office today, couldn't concentrate. You see, as of last week . . . well, Max and I were not exactly on good terms."

"God! I hope he'll be okay."

"So do I," Freddie said dryly. "Because if Max dies, everyone will say I put a hit on him. That would go nicely with my reputation. Right?"

"How can you be so cynical?" she said, wondering why he would even say such a thing.

"Let's make a deal, Madison. Unless I signal that you can put your tape on, *anything* I say is completely off the record. Agreed?"

"I'll go with that."

"Excellent decision."

She shook her head. "This is a very violent town."

"Where are *you* from?"

"New York."

"And I suppose New York isn't violent?"

"I've been here three days, and already Salli T. Turner's been murdered, and now Max Steele has been shot."

"Read the papers, something happens every day."

"Was he at home?"

"No, the police say it was a robbery in a parking lot. Apparently somebody wanted his Rolex." Freddie sighed. "Do you *know* how many times I've warned him not to walk around with a seventeen-thousand-dollar gold watch on his wrist?"

Madison wanted to respond, "How about you in your two-hundred-and-fifty-thousand-dollar car?" But she did the prudent thing and resisted. "Will you be able to *keep* it out of the news?" she asked.

"I doubt it."

"And you say your wife is at the hospital with him?"

"Diana took it badly. I never realized they were so close."

Hmm, Madison thought, *there's a telling remark.*

"You'll have to excuse me," Freddie continued. "My head's not in a good place right now. When I left the hospital last night I took a ride to the beach. We have a small house there which nobody ever uses. It's the only place I can relax. I enjoy solitude."

"So do I."

"I'll lend you the keys one day."

"I'll take you up on that. I love the beach," Madison said, thinking that Freddie Leon was not at all like his reputation. This titan of the big deal seemed lonely and almost vulnerable.

They rode in silence for a while.

"Y'know," Madison said. "The last thing I want is to hassle you. So if this isn't a good time, we don't *have* to talk today—we could get together next week."

"I like you," Freddie said, ignoring her offer. "I knew that the moment you walked into my office. Believe me—I don't say that to many people."

"I'm flattered."

"Madison—interesting name."

"My parents met on Madison Avenue," she said lightly. "My mother was shopping, and I guess my father was looking."

"Your parents still alive?"

"They live in Connecticut, moved out of the city last year."

"Smart. That's exactly what I plan on doing eventually—buy myself an old farmhouse in France and give all this up."

"You'd relinquish all your power and leave L.A.?"

"In a moment," he said, making a sharp turn onto Melrose.

"Where are we going?" she asked, peering out the window.

"My secret place," he said. "Only it's not so secret with the tourists. It's somewhere I don't have other agents and producers begging for favors. Also, they serve the best Danish in the city."

"Where's that?"

"Farmer's Market on Fairfax."

Her eyebrows rose. "Farmer's Market?"

"You'll love it," he assured her.

"I will?"

"Yes, Madison, you will."

She settled back in the passenger seat. This meeting was turning out to be much more interesting than she'd expected.

chapter 7

DIANA SAT BESIDE MAX Steele's hospital bed. He was still unconscious and in intensive care, but the doctors had told her he had a good chance of making it. She hoped and prayed it was true, because if he survived, she definitely had decided to tell Freddie she was leaving him.

Of course, there was one small snag. When she and Max had met for breakfast, he'd revealed that he had just gotten engaged, and she—like a fool—had later shared the news with Freddie. When Freddie left the hospital last night, he'd instructed her to contact Max's fiancée immediately.

She had not done so. Why should she? It seemed unnecessary. She was perfectly happy sitting next to Max, watching over him. The last thing she needed was a stupid fiancée getting in her way. For a brief moment she'd considered calling Max's secretary at home to get the girl's number, but then it had seemed more sensible to wait until the next day.

Now it was Monday morning and she finally realized she'd better call the girl or Freddie would throw a fit. He was a stickler for getting his own way. It irked her, but there seemed to be no other choice.

She called Max's secretary, Meg, who sounded completely devastated. "When can I come to the hospital?" Meg asked, choking back tears.

"Not yet, dear," Diana responded.

"Everyone at the office is so concerned," Meg continued. "Mr. Leon called a staff meeting this morning and told us all. Oh, Mrs. Leon, it's such a shock. What can I do?"

"I need the number of a friend of Mr. Steele's," Diana said crisply, unable to bring herself to say "fiancée."

"Of course, Mrs. Leon—who would that be?"

"Her name's Kristin something. I don't have a last name."

"Hold on a moment, I'll look in the book."

Diana held on impatiently. It was obvious Meg knew nothing about a fiancée. Good.

Finally Meg returned. "I can't seem to find a listing in the business book for a Kristin. However, his personal phone book is on his desk. Would you like me to take a look in that?"

For a moment Diana was tempted to say no. If she was unable to get the girl's number she couldn't inform her. "Very well," she said at last.

Meg left her hanging again and returned a moment later. "Since we have no last name I'll look under the K's," she said. "Ah yes, there *is* a Kristin listed.

Kristin, and in brackets, Darlene, then there's a number."

"Give it to me," Diana said impatiently.

"Yes, Mrs. Leon. Is there anything else I can do? Maybe bring some of his clothes to the hospital? Or drop by his house?"

"Good idea, Meg. Go to his house and warn the housekeeper that if anyone comes to the door, not to say a word. We're trying to keep this quiet."

"There're spies in all the hospitals, Mrs. Leon," Meg said. She was an avid reader of the tabloids.

"I know, dear. Which is exactly why we've hired security."

Diana did not call immediately, but waited another half hour before reluctantly dialing the number Meg had given her.

An uptight-sounding woman answered.

"Is this Kristin?" Diana said, equally uptight.

"Who *is* this?" the woman demanded, her voice shrill and angry.

"Mrs. Freddie Leon," Diana said haughtily.

"There's no Kristin here."

"Is this Darlene?"

"Are you from the media?"

"Ex*cuse* me?"

"Don't bother me at home again," the woman shrieked. "Call my lawyer. I'm suing every one of you. You people make me *sick.*"

And with that the woman slammed the phone down, leaving Diana stunned.

chapter 8

Now THAT HIS FATHER WAS safely married for the fourth time, Jake Sica decided he'd done his duty by attending the wedding, and now it was time to start getting *his* life together. Since arriving in L.A. from his home base in Arizona barely a week ago, so much had happened, and he'd been so preoccupied that he'd done nothing about finding an apartment, let alone checking in with the magazine he was about to start taking pictures for. Which was kind of stupid, because until he let them know he was in L.A. and ready to work, there would be no weekly paycheck coming his way. And although he was an award-winning photographer, he was not exactly rolling in bucks. Which is one of the reasons he'd decided to take the highly paid magazine job in L.A.

He sat in a coffee shop on Sunset toying with a late breakfast of bacon and eggs, ruminating his fate, and wondering why it was his luck to have met a gorgeous delectable woman—with whom he'd fallen instantly in love, not to mention lust—who then turned out to be an extremely highly paid call girl. Goddamn it! The whole scenario was like a bad movie.

Last night he'd had dinner with his new best friend, Madison, and she'd advised him to call Kristin and hear her side of things. He'd done so, but Kristin was out, so he'd left a long message on her answering machine. So far she hadn't responded.

He had a feeling she might have been sitting beside her machine listening to him and hating him because he'd walked out on her when he'd found out the shattering truth.

Fuck! He'd blown it. He should at least have stayed around long enough to listen to what she had to say. Instead he'd marched out like an insulted virgin, yelling something like, "Why didn't you tell me? I would've worn a condom."

Jesus! Talk about bad behavior.

After brooding over his coffee, he finally went to a pay phone and tried again to reach Kristin.

This time a female voice answered, only it wasn't Kristin—it sounded more like a foreign maid. "Kristin?" he asked hopefully, even though he knew it wasn't her.

"No, this Chiew. I take message?"

"Uh . . . I need to talk to the lady you work for. Will she be back soon?"

"Don't know. Madam not come home last night."

Oh, that was great. She was probably out with a big-bucks client having wild, paid-for sex.

"What time *will* she be home?"

"No, sorry."

He gave her his number at the hotel, impressing upon her that it was urgent Kristin call him the moment she came in. He didn't know what else to do, but he *did* know it was imperative that he talk to her as soon as possible so that he could try to straighten things out.

He went back to his table, finished his coffee, paid the check and strode out into the hot noon sun.

In her office at the TV station, Natalie De Barge was busy working on what could turn out to be the biggest story of her career, and it wasn't about Salli T. Turner. The lead had been handed to her by her news director, Garth, who had a loyal spy in the police department. She'd taken the small amount of information he'd given her and run with it.

Natalie was well aware that this was her big opportunity to get out of boring show-business gossip and into hard news. This was her chance to shine with a *real* story. She, Natalie De Barge, was about to become famous.

She'd been working on her story all night, and now she had it together in time for the noon news.

As she sat at her computer finishing up, Jimmy Sica, the good-looking news anchor with the dazzling smile, wandered over and stood behind her. "I hear you got a hot deal goin', babe," he said, rubbing her shoulders.

"That's right, Jimmy," she replied, shrugging his hands off her back.

"Y'know," he said casually. "Garth and I were talking, and although your story's kind of showbiz-related, he thought *I* should be the one to break it."

She turned around and stared up at him. "You've

gotta be kidding. This is *my* story, Jimmy. *Mine.* I worked on this all damn night and all morning, and I am *not* giving it up to *anyone."*

"But it'll be stronger coming from me," Jimmy pointed out.

"What's *wrong* with Garth?" Natalie snapped, her eyes flashing major danger signals. "He didn't have the balls to tell me himself?"

"Guess he knew you'd be mad," Jimmy said weakly.

"Fuck him and fuck you, Jimmy," she said furiously. "I'm on air with this. Don't mess with me."

"No need to get nasty," he said, backing off, a hurt expression on his handsome face.

"If *you* had a great exclusive, wouldn't *you* be angry?"

"I'm only trying to be helpful."

She narrowed her eyes. "In what way?"

"You're not used to presenting hard news. You do the trivia—who's sleeping with whom—the Leonardo DiCaprio and Gwyneth Paltrow shit."

"Yes. And that's *exactly* what I'm trying to get away from. *This* is my opportunity."

"Okay, okay, don't get your panties caught up your butt," Jimmy said, rapidly backing off. "I'll tell Garth."

"Yeah, and while you're doing that, tell him the *next* time he has something to say to me, he can do it himself."

Jimmy mock-saluted. "Got it."

Natalie was fuming. She should've known that Garth wanted *her* to do the work, while Jimmy took all the glory. It was always that way.

But they weren't getting away with it this time. This story was *definitely* hers.

chapter 9

"**I**'M COMPLETELY DISARMED," Madison said, brushing a lock of dark hair out of her eyes.

They were sitting outside at Farmer's Market eating Danish and sipping iced tea.

Freddie leaned across the small table. "What was that?" he said.

She laughed, "I *said*, I'm completely disarmed by you. You're nothing at all like your public image."

"Yes, but we'll keep that between us, won't we?"

"In everything I've read about you, you come across as a cold power broker with a heart of stone. A man who's only interested in mega deals. Are you aware that everybody's scared of you? Yet here *I* am, a journalist of all people, sitting here with you having an exceptionally pleasant time."

"Glad to hear it," he said, sipping his iced tea. "As I

told you before, you caught me on a strange day." For a moment he paused, staring reflectively into the distance. "You see, yesterday I thought I wanted nothing more to do with Max Steele. And today I keep thinking about how we both started out together, our close friendship, the way we built our agency from nothing. Max was the personality, I was the brains. Not that I'm saying Max doesn't have brains. He's a hard worker and street smart—qualities I admire."

"I only met him briefly," Madison said, remembering Max climbing into his pristine red Maserati with a big smile on his face. "However, I must say I liked him. He's a complete egomaniac, but an unabashed one—which gives him a certain amount of charm."

"How did you meet him?" Freddie asked curiously.

"My girlfriend's brother, Cole, arranged it so that we bumped into each other jogging. He knew I wanted to ask Max about you."

"And how does Cole know Max?"

"Cole's a personal trainer. In fact, I think he's worked *you* out a couple of times. Black guy, very good-looking."

"Diana hires the trainers."

"I get the picture. Your wife runs your personal life. You run the business."

He threw her one of his cold looks. "I can assure you, Madison, my personal life is all mine."

Hmm, she thought, *mustn't go too far; this is an interesting, complex man, and I should hold back.* "So far you haven't allowed me to put on my tape recorder," she said, hoping he might acquiesce. "Which means I have no interview."

"That's all right," Freddie said, taking another sip

of iced tea. "As I told you before, we must get to know each other first before I subject myself."

"But this would be so perfect to write about," she said enthusiastically. "The real Freddie Leon. The man who actually bleeds if he's cut."

"Maybe it's the perfect interview for *you*," he said evenly. "However, it is not quite the image *I* wish to present to the world."

She fixed him with a long look. "When *do* I get to put on my tape?"

"Maybe later in the week I'll take you to lunch and give you the official interview, the one I've never given before."

"Sounds good to me."

He offered a glimmer of a smile. "I'll tell you how Max and I started out, all about our first clients, the people we've dealt with over the years. I'll give you a good interview. But today I feel like forgetting about everything. You can understand that, can't you?"

"As a matter of fact, I *do* know how you feel," she said, nodding vigorously. "When Salli Turner got murdered I was in shock, and it's only been a couple of days."

"Was she a friend of yours?"

"An acquaintance. I'm going to her funeral later. Did *you* know her?"

He shook his head. "No."

She remembered Salli telling her about how she'd met Freddie in the underground garage of his building. Probably he was stalked by so many would-be actresses that he genuinely didn't remember.

"Where's the funeral?" he asked.

"Westwood," she replied. "Cole's taking me, he knew Salli pretty well."

"It seems Cole knows everyone."

"He does. And all their secrets, too. Sort of like you, although on a different level." She took a big bite of Danish; Freddie was right, it was delicious. "Who do *you* think murdered Salli?"

Freddie paused before answering. "Difficult to know with these girls," he said slowly. "They arrive in town with nothing but their looks and a whole lot of ambition. Then, if they're lucky, they make a little money, get a touch of fame, and that's when they all pick the wrong man. They're incapable of dating anyone with substance. I've seen it happen a thousand times. We have a girl at our agency, Angela Musconni. She's a wonderful young actress, yet there's something about her—something I know will eventually destroy her—one way or the other."

"Must be tough for you to watch. Can we talk about that?"

"Don't push it, Madison," he said shortly.

She pushed it anyway. "I was thinking of interviewing your secretary, maybe your wife, and some of your friends," she said. "Would that bother you?"

"When I'm ready, I'll give you the list of who you can talk to," he said abruptly.

"You're very controlling, Freddie."

"The secret of my success, Madison."

"Okay," she said, sighing. "The rules are yours, so I guess I'm going to have to play the game your way."

"Good. Because otherwise you'd be out of the ballpark."

An hour later he dropped her off in the underground parking garage at his building. "Call me tomorrow," he said.

"Will I get past the dreaded Ria?"

"If you're persistent."

"Gee, thanks."

She collected her car from the valet and drove home.

"Am I glad you're here," Cole said, greeting her at the door. "Natalie called—she's breakin' a big story on the noon news, wants me to tape it. You got any idea how to work this goddamn machine?"

"Put in a tape, and press Record."

"I don't have to set it?"

"C'mon, Cole—of course not. When you play it back, you merely fast-forward to where you want to go."

"Hey—very smart."

"What's Nat's story about?" Madison asked, opening the fridge and taking out a bottle of Evian.

"The Malibu blonde deal. She's been working it all night."

"What happened with Luther?" Madison asked, swigging from the bottle.

"She gave him up for her story."

"Natalie putting work before a guy? Now *that's* progress." They both laughed. "What time should we leave for Salli's funeral?"

"Soon as we've watched big Sis. We should get there early."

"Good."

"How'd it go with Freddie?"

"He's quite an amazing man," Madison said thoughtfully. "With a great deal of personal integrity."

Cole raised an eyebrow. "Never heard *that* about

Freddie Leon. Around town they call him the Snake—y'know, he'll bite you soon as look at you."

"You're a cynic, Cole."

"Takes one to know one," he said, turning on the TV and fiddling with the tape machine.

"I have bad news," Madison said, flopping down on the couch. "The story hasn't broken yet, but Max Steele was shot in a robbery yesterday."

"Whaaat?"

"He's in intensive care. *Don't* spread the news; I was told in confidence."

"Anythin' we can do?"

"Guess not."

Cole shook his head and turned the sound up on the TV as Jimmy Sica appeared on screen and began reading the current news.

"Jimmy's one good-lookin' dude," he commented.

"And straight, too," Madison murmured dryly.

"A guy can fantasize, can't he?"

"Personally I think his brother Jake's more attractive. Jake doesn't realize how sexy and handsome he is. Jimmy does. He probably spends most of his life admiring himself in front of a mirror."

"That's 'cause he's on TV," Cole pointed out. "The dude *has* t' look good."

"Jake would get *my* vote any day."

"Gotta feelin' you're into him, huh?" Cole teased.

"We're friends, that's all," Madison said defensively. "As I told you last night, the man is taken."

"That, sugar pie, would *never* stop me," Cole said with a wicked grin.

"Hey, if a guy is bagged, it's okay with me—I can walk away."

41

Natalie appeared on screen. "The sister's lookin' fine!" Cole exclaimed proudly.

"She sure is," Madison agreed, impressed with Natalie's businesslike image: a black Armani suit with a white silk shirt, and no outrageous jewelry—Natalie's usual trademark.

"Good evening," Natalie said, poised and in control. "Natalie De Barge reporting." A short dramatic pause. "Hollywood. Land of dreams. A fantasy paradise where anything can happen, and sometimes does. Yesterday a young girl's body washed up on the Malibu shore. We were all quick to christen her the Malibu Mystery Blonde—after all, this *is* L.A., land of the instant sound bite, and we—the media—go with it every time. What could be better? A beautiful young blond female to titillate our thirst for the latest headline. But *our* Mystery Malibu Blonde has a name. She was nineteen-year-old Hildie Jane Livins from Idaho. Hildie came to L.A. three years ago, just like thousands of other young hopefuls with starry eyes and Hollywood dreams."

The camera cut to a medium shot of a plain-faced woman in a print dress standing outside a remote farmhouse. "Hilda was a good girl," the woman said. "I lived next door to her family going on thirteen years. She was a pretty little thing. Never gave no one no trouble. Minded her own business an' helped her mom around the house."

The camera cut back to Natalie. "In Hollywood Hildie tried to make it in show business. She got a job working as a checkout girl in a supermarket, attended acting class, and hung out with her friends who were also trying to make it. Mavis Ann Fenwick was Hildie's roommate for two years."

Cut to shot of a skinny brunette with a big ass. She was standing on a Hollywood street, dressed in shorts and a T-shirt. "Hildie was the coolest," Mavis Ann said, blinking nervously. "We always had fun, and when things weren't going good, she *never* complained." A manic giggle. "Once we lived on Campbell's soup for three solid weeks 'cause we couldn't afford nothin' else."

Camera back to Natalie in the studio. "Eventually the temptations of Hollywood lured Hildie into a life of decadence," Natalie continued. "This innocent young girl met a sophisticated worldly-wise woman who goes by the name of Darlene La Porte. Darlene's real name is Pat Smithins—a former convicted prostitute who has also been arrested several times for pandering. According to Mavis Ann and other friends of Hildie's, Darlene promised Hildie money and acting opportunities if she agreed to sleep with movie stars and rich men. Darlene, in fact, became Hildie's madam." A long pause. "Now Hildie is dead, murdered by drowning and dumped in the ocean to make it look like an accident. When we tried to reach Darlene La Porte for her comments, we were informed she had nothing to say. Tell *that* to Hildie's grieving parents."

"Jesus!" Cole exclaimed, leaping up. "Whaddya think?"

"I think it's damn good investigative reporting," Madison said. "I only hope she has plenty of hard facts to back up her story, because Darlene whatever her name is will have her lawyers crawling all over everyone."

Cole grabbed his jacket. "Come on," he said. "We got a funeral to attend."

chapter 10

KRISTIN WAS DESPERATELY
trying to keep it together, but it was getting difficult.
She was naked and alone, locked in a boarded-up
room with no bathroom, she had no food or water,
and although she was desperately trying not to panic,
it had already occurred to her that maybe Mister X
might *not* return.

The thought sent tingles of fear up and down her
spine. Nobody knew where she was or with whom
she'd had a date. Mister X had booked her directly,
and like a fool—because she was upset and disappointed about the Jake situation and Max not keeping
their appointment—she'd gone.

Stupid little whore. You're getting what you deserve.

She attempted to shut off the inner voice that
screamed in her head. The voice that always spoke the
painful truth.

44

The light seeping through the boarded-up window was stronger now. It must be at least noon, she thought, and still there was no Mister X.

The sick degenerate son of a bitch. Her greed had led her to him. Her greed would be her downfall. And yet all she'd really wanted to do was make sure Cherie was taken care of. Was that so terrible?

Cherie. What would happen to her if Kristin wasn't there to pay the bills? Oh God! They'd switch off the machines keeping her alive. Oh God!

With a sudden burst of strength Kristin hurled herself against the door like she'd seen heroes do in movies.

It didn't budge. She wasn't a hero. She wasn't even a heroine. She was just a lonely whore locked in a room with an envelope filled with cash.

I'm going to die in this room. The thought seemed to hover over her like a black shroud.

She slumped to the floor. And then she screamed— a long, piercing wail of a scream.

But there was no one around to hear.

chapter 11

CAPTAIN MARSH WAS yelling about the news story on the Mystery Malibu Blonde. "Where'd they get their information?" he shouted. "We only just identified the girl. How come they're on air with a full story before we gave out an official statement?"

Tucci shrugged. "I got a funeral to go to, Captain. Can we get into this when I come back?"

"No!" Marsh snarled. "Where's this Darlene woman? I want her questioned pronto."

"We've already contacted her lawyer. He's agreed to bring her in later to answer some questions. We had to put on the pressure. She apparently has . . . connections."

"Fuck this shit!" Marsh stormed. "Salli T. Turner. Now, this. I need some fuckin' arrests around here."

Tucci stifled a yawn. "Yes, sir."

"Where's Eccles?"

"Questioning the lap-dancers who flew back with Bobby Skorch."

"He would be," Captain Marsh growled.

Tucci glanced at his watch. "I don't want to be late—"

"Get the fuck outta here."

Tucci was only too glad to leave. He felt like crap. Hungry. Tired. Overworked. There'd been a spate of murders over the last month. He'd been lucky enough not to have pulled duty on any of them—but now this.

Faye said it was a good thing. "You'll solve them," she'd told him in a quietly confident voice. "You're the best."

It was nice to have a woman who believed in him all the way.

On his way to Salli T. Turner's funeral, he stopped at a Winchell's and bought three glazed chocolate donuts. Faye's disapproving face flashed into his brain. Jesus! It wasn't as if he'd had time for lunch. The donuts were in *place* of lunch—a poor substitute, but certainly better than nothing.

Meanwhile, in a luxury hotel on Sunset, Lee Eccles knocked on the door of Suite 300 and prepared to interview the two lap-dancers/strippers who'd flown to L.A. with Bobby Skorch. He'd tracked the limo driver, who told him where he'd deposited Bobby and the girls.

The two women answered the door together. Lee flashed his badge and informed them he was there on official business. They mentioned they were about to take off on a shopping spree, but at his insistence they reluctantly backed into the untidy suite and he followed them in.

Their names were Gospel and Tuscany, both blondes, both stacked. Gospel, who was clad in a red cat suit with several gold crosses hanging round her neck and two giant crosses hanging from her ears, had long, straight hair down to her waist. She was stoned.

Tuscany, pneumatic body poured into a crotch-skimming leopard skin dress and hooker heels, had short bubble-cut hair.

"This won't take long," Lee said, checking out the spacious suite which was costing *somebody* a buck or two. "I only have a few questions."

"Don't you need a warrant t'do this?" Tuscany said, obviously the brighter of the two.

"Want me to get one?" Lee countered, shooting her his best "I'm a cop—get outta my face" look.

"If it's about that old guy in Vegas," Gospel interrupted, feigning outrage. "Wasn't *my* fault he had a heart attack. Dunno *why* his old cow of a wife is suing me. You from the insurance company?"

"No, he's not from the insurance company," Tuscany said irritably. "He's a cop. Didn't you see his badge?"

"Cop, insurance company—all the same to me," Gospel said, absentmindedly stroking her left nipple through the thin material of her cat suit.

"What do you want anyway?" Tuscany demanded, staring him in the eye.

Lee didn't answer for a moment. He was fantasizing about how they'd be girl on girl. Pretty raunchy if he knew his women. Yes, this was definitely a dynamic duo. "You flew into L.A. Saturday night with Bobby Skorch, is that right?" he asked, eyeballing Gospel's ample cleavage.

"Who told you that?" Tuscany said suspiciously, tugging down her leopard skirt.

"The Secret Service," Lee drawled sarcastically.

"Bobby said we weren't supposed to tell anybody," Gospel whined.

"Why you wanna know?" Tuscany demanded.

"Routine," Lee said. "Did Bobby give you money?"

"Whaddya think we are—hookers?" Gospel said, clearly insulted.

"Not at all," Lee said with a smirk. "I know you're two nice young ladies who simply happen to strip for a living—right? You make a buck here, a buck there. Why not? If you've got it, show it."

"We're good at what we do," Gospel said defensively. "That's why Bobby chose to fly *us* to L.A. with him, and not any of those other bitches."

"After you got off the plane Saturday night, what happened?" Lee asked. The limo driver had already told him he'd driven all three of them to the hotel, but he wanted to hear their version.

Gospel giggled. "What *didn't* happen?"

"You came directly to the hotel?"

"Yeah, we came straight here," Tuscany said. "So what?"

"Can you recall what time you arrived?"

"Dunno," Gospel said with a careless shrug. "Maybe seven or eight. We had a coupla shots, then Bobby hadda go out."

Tuscany shot her a warning look.

"He told us not to tell anybody that either," Gospel added lamely. "Said we was to say we were with him all night."

"Aren't you supposed to give us a warning or something?" Tuscany said. "You know, like one of those 'anything you say may be used as evidence against you' kinds of deals. That's what cops do in the movies."

"That's only if I'm planning on arresting you," Lee said. "Which I'm not."

"Ooh, good, I'm so relieved," Tuscany said sarcastically.

It was as if neither of them knew what was going on. "You *do* know about the murder?" he said, exasperated.

"What murder?" Gospel said, her eyes widening.

"Salli T. Turner."

"Horrible!" Gospel squeaked. "We watched some of the coverage stuff on TV."

"And you *do* know that Salli was Bobby Skorch's wife?"

Both girls went into dumb overdrive.

"Didn't know that," Tuscany said.

"Me neither," Gospel said.

"Didn't even know he was married," Tuscany added.

These girls were plain stupid, but then he hadn't expected a couple of Einsteins. "So, ladies," he said, "you'd better think *very* carefully about what you're about to tell me and be completely honest about it. Because otherwise, you girls could find yourself in a shit-load of trouble. Get it?"

chapter 12

OUTSIDE PIERCE BROTH-
ers cemetery in Westwood there was a line of limos
and cars stretching for blocks. It was always that way
at a celebrity funeral. In Hollywood, celebrity funerals were regarded as an event—people attended them
to be seen; it validated their very existence.

Tucci bypassed the line, showing his badge to
security, who waved him by. He'd devoured all three
donuts on the way there, and now he felt bloated and
guilty. If Faye knew what he'd eaten for lunch she'd
kill him. *Maybe death's better than deprivation,* he
thought with the shadow of a smile.

He fell in with the other guests entering the already
overcrowded chapel. Although he was early, there
were only a few places left. He recognized the journalist who had brought him the audiotape of Salli. She

JACKIE COLLINS

was sitting near the back, so he quickly slid in beside her.

"Good afternoon, Detective Tucci," Madison said, turning to give him a quick once-over.

He acknowledged her with a nod, unable to recall her name—which infuriated him because he was good at remembering names, although in the last few months this had happened to him several times. A couple of weeks ago he'd complained to Faye. His wife had prodded him gently in the stomach and said teasingly, or so he'd thought, "Alzheimer's. You're nearly fifty, you know."

Screw nearly fifty. He was forty-nine years old, he had another ten months to go before he was fifty. Sometimes Faye exhibited an uncharacteristic mean streak.

"Miss Castelli—Madison," he almost shouted, so happy was he to suddenly remember her name.

"Yes?" she said, startled.

"Uh . . . how did the piece you were about to write on Salli turn out?"

"I've done better," she said wryly.

"I'm sure it was excellent," he responded. "My wife raves about your work. Reads your magazine every month."

"Thank you," she said with a pleased smile.

Tucci considered Madison Castelli to be a very beautiful woman with her dark hair and almond-shaped eyes—not to mention her lips, which gave "seductive" a whole new meaning. Not that he was interested in other women, but he could look and admire, couldn't he?

He leaned forward to see who she was with.

"Hey, man," Cole said, noticing he was getting checked out. "How ya doin'?"

Tucci nodded briefly and leaned back. Then he began surveying the room, noting one famous face after the other. Faye would have a great time here; she loved stars and gossip, her one failing.

"This is so very sad," Madison sighed, shaking her head. "I still can't believe it."

"I know," he agreed.

"Do you have any leads?"

"We'll be making a statement soon."

"Was my tape helpful?"

"Yes, ma'am."

All of a sudden raucous old-fashioned rock and roll began blaring through the speakers, silencing any further conversation. Mick Jagger. Metallica. Rod Stewart. Kiss.

Tucci thought his eardrums might burst. Funerals today—you couldn't trust 'em.

Eddie Stoner insisted they attend Salli's funeral, and Angie didn't argue. After all, she was in his bed again, why shouldn't she go along with what he wanted to do? If she'd been working, it might have saved her from falling back into his life, but her new movie didn't start shooting for six weeks so she had plenty of time to play.

Her immediate problem was Kevin. What to do about Kevin? By this time he must have realized something was amiss since she'd run out in the middle of the night. She knew she had to call him eventually, and she did so reluctantly when she was in the car on the way to the funeral. "Uh . . . listen,

Kev," she said cheerfully when he answered. "Somethin' came up."

"Where the *fuck* have you been?" Kevin exploded; he sounded like he'd been waiting by the phone.

"I bumped into an old friend, and uh . . . I won't be back till later."

"Later when?"

"Dunno," she said evasively.

"Hey—" he said furiously. "How about not bothering to come back at all?"

"Go screw yourself," she said, her temper rising. "It's my house, too. I paid half the money."

"Y'know, Angie, this isn't working for me," Kevin said grimly.

"Not working for *you*," she said indignantly. *"I'm* the one who's checking out."

"Oh, you're leaving? Good. *I'll* keep the house."

"No freakin' way," she objected, her voice getting shriller by the minute. "We bought the house together, remember?"

"Tell you what," Kevin said, relieved to have this sudden escape hatch. "I'll call *my* lawyer, you call *yours*—let *them* work it out. Right now I don't want to see you here."

"You don't get it," Angie yelled. *"I* don't want to see *you* there. Anyway," she added, lowering her voice, suddenly remembering that Eddie was sitting right beside her. "I can't talk about it now. I'm on my way to Salli's funeral."

"Oh, your good friend Salli," Kevin jeered. "Isn't that the girl you used to nonstop trash?"

"Can't you speak well of the dead?" Angie said contemptuously.

"Goodbye," Kevin said, and hung up.

Eddie, who was pretending to concentrate on driving her Ferrari, stared straight ahead. "Problems?" he said, casually patting her on the knee.

"I was plannin' on dumpin' him anyway," Angie muttered. "His ego's bustin' out all over. The asshole's startin' to believe his own publicity. Jerk! Some people can't handle stardom."

"Not like you, huh?" Eddie said, tossing back his luxuriant mane of dirty blond hair.

"I handle it, ace," Angie boasted. "All these sex-crazed producers tryin' to jump me. Not that I'm exactly Miss Sex Symbol 1998, but they're horny dogs—they all wanna know if they can still get it up. Ha! Dumb old cockers—they pop Viagra with their morning coffee. Think gettin' a boner makes 'em more of a man."

"Now, now," Eddie said, laughing to himself. "Don't go gettin' bitter on me."

When the car turned off Wilshire Boulevard, Eddie immediately noticed a long line of limos ahead of them. "We should've taken a car and driver," he moaned. "This is gonna be a rat fuck."

"Thought you *wanted* to drive the Ferrari," Angie retorted, her mind still half focused on Kevin.

"I did," he said, opening the window, leaning out, and attracting the attention of a young Hispanic traffic cop. "Hey, excuse me, friend. I've got Angela Musconni in the car. She's tryin' to avoid gettin' mobbed or set upon by the photographers. Anything you can do for us?"

"Sure, man," the cop said, attempting to peer into the passenger seat and take a good look at Angie, whom he'd recently seen in a movie where she'd strutted around half naked. "Leave your car. I'll get a parking valet to take it. You can sneak her in through the back."

"'Preciate it," Eddie said.

"Very smooth," Angie said, jumping out of the car.

"Yeah, well, don't see why my darling should wait around," said Eddie. Then he leaned over and gave her a long, slow French kiss.

Angie surfaced with a stupid grin on her face.

It was great being back with Eddie, especially now that *she* was in the boss position.

chapter 13

"I'M SUING EVERY SINGLE stinking one of them. I'm suing that black bitch, *and* the TV station, and anyone else who dares cross me."

"Calm down," said Darlene La Porte's lawyer, Linden Masters, a tall man with piercing blue eyes and a distinguished white beard. Linden had an air of respectability about him, which went down well with judges, considering he represented some of the most notorious people in Hollywood, including Darlene, who'd come to him when she'd grown tired of using cut-price lawyers, and had realized that paying for the best got her the services she required.

"That bitch practically accused me of *killing* Hildie," Darlene fumed. "I know *nothing* about it."

"Which is exactly why we're visiting the police station later today," Linden said in an irritatingly calm voice. "You'll tell them you don't know anything, after which they'll leave you alone. Cooperation is the key. If you avoid speaking to them, Darlene, they'll think you have something to hide."

"What do you mean?" she asked crossly.

Linden pulled on his beard. *"Did* you send Hildie out to meet a client?"

"No," Darlene said, pacing up and down the thick pile carpet in her luxurious living room.

"You're sure? Because if you did, you'd better tell *me.* As your lawyer I'm here to protect you. And if you're concealing any evidence at all . . ."

"Oh, God, Linden," she said, collapsing into an overstuffed armchair. "Of course I'm not." What she really wanted to say was "Yes, I sent her out with the one client I know nothing about. He calls himself Mister X. I hear from him only occasionally. He pays big bucks. All cash. The girls think he's weird, but he's never done any of them harm." But, of course, she said no such thing.

"Good," Linden said.

Darlene jumped up and walked over to the large picture window overlooking Wilshire Boulevard. She gazed out, watching the cars race by at great speed. For a moment her mind drifted back to a year ago and Kimberly. She'd fixed Kimberly up with a client. That client was Mister X. A week later the girl's body was fished out of the ocean.

In her mind Darlene had always refused to connect the two, imagining Kimberly had gone off with her friends *after* her appointment with Mister X, and died or been murdered at one of the drug parties she always hung out at. Now this.

"I *help* these girls," she said, speaking rapidly. "If I

wasn't around to supervise their lives they'd be out on the street or mud wrestling in some seedy place by the freeway. *I* save them from themselves. Thanks to me they live in nice apartments, wear beautiful clothes. I'm *good* for them."

"You don't have to tell me," Linden said, sure that Darlene believed her own lies. But as long as she paid his exorbitant bills, what did *he* care?

"What will this do to my reputation?" she wailed, turning toward him. *"Can* I sue? I have no desire to become another Heidi Fleiss."

"There's not much chance of that," Linden said. "They caught Heidi on alleged tax evasion. You *pay* your taxes."

"Yes, yes, I'm a good citizen," Darlene said, convincing herself that she was. "I own a successful flower shop, which is where my income comes from. And I pay plenty of taxes. *Plenty.* Now my reputation has been besmirched and I want retribution."

"Don't worry," Linden said. "We'll get it. But you've got to remember, Darlene, you *do* have a record, and that's *not* in your favor."

"Dammit, Linden," she snapped. "I pay you a lot of money to keep my reputation clean."

"I'll be back to fetch you in two hours," Linden said, anxious to escape her bad mood. "In the meantime, don't speak to anyone. No public comments. Tell your service to handle all calls."

"Very well."

Darlene saw Linden to the door and went into her bedroom. Hildie had been such a sweet, fun-loving girl, almost innocent in a way. *Why* had she sent her out with Mister X? She knew the man was a pervert.

Why hadn't she chosen one of her more sophisticated girls? Then she remembered, it was Kristin he'd wanted.

Impulsively she went to the phone and dialed Kristin's number. The maid informed her she was out. "I need to speak to her urgently, Chiew," Darlene said.

"I sorry," Chiew replied. "Miss Kristin no come home last night. I worried. No message, nothing."

"Didn't come home?" Darlene said, panic suddenly rising. It wasn't like Kristin to vanish without leaving word where she was—she always made sure she was reachable in case there was an emergency concerning her sister. "Do you know where she went?" Darlene asked, attempting to remain unruffled.

"No, ma'am. A gentleman called. Jake Sica. When she come back, he want her to phone him at hotel."

"Give me his number," Darlene said abruptly. "And when she does come home, have her call me immediately."

Darlene looked at the number as she put down the phone. She had a bad feeling, a very bad feeling. Who was this Jake? Kristin didn't go out unless it was business. She'd confided to Darlene that she had no need of a personal life, all that concerned her was making enough money to take care of her sister.

Picking up the phone, Darlene quickly called the number. It was a hotel. "Jake Sica," she said, trying to get her mind around the name which sounded vaguely familiar.

He answered on the first ring.

"I understand you're looking for Kristin," Darlene said.

Jake immediately recognized the woman's distinctive voice from Kristin's answering machine. "Who's this?" he asked.

"It doesn't matter who I am. Do you know where Kristin is?"

"You're her madam, aren't you?"

"Excuse me?"

"I was there when you called on her machine. You wanted her to meet a Mister X. You said he'd pay her a lot of money."

"Who the hell are you?" Darlene screeched, blowing her usual cool.

"Somebody who cares about her."

"If you care about her so much, how come you don't know where she spent last night?"

"Not that it's any of your business, but we got into a fight because of your message. Now I'm looking for her, too."

Darlene slammed the phone down. She wasn't about to get involved. This could only lead to trouble.

Lurking outside the bedroom, Junia Ladd, Darlene's significant other, had been listening to the conversation with her ear pressed close to the door. Junia, a pointy-faced girl of eighteen, with delicate ivory skin and wispy fair hair, had been Darlene's live-in lover for eighteen months, ever since Darlene had rescued her from a juvenile detention center.

Junia enjoyed the luxury of living with Darlene, but sometimes she had to break free, and when she did, she needed extra money. Making something on the side was most desirable, because although Darlene was generous, she always had to know exactly how Junia spent her money. Junia could go into Sak's or Neiman's and charge whatever she wished, but if Darlene suspected she was out spending her money on grass or coke, she threw a nasty fit.

Sometimes Junia stole the odd hundred from Darlene's Prada purse when she thought she could get away with it. Other times she tried to do people favors in return for cash. Giving Mister X Kristin's number was a favor for which she'd gotten paid five hundred bucks. Luckily Darlene had been in the bathroom when she'd answered the phone. It was Mister X tracking Kristin. He must have sensed Junia was someone he could manipulate, because the first thing he'd said was "Give me Kristin's home number and I'll pay *you* five hundred bucks."

"How do I know you'll do that?" Junia had said, glancing at the bathroom door, making sure that Darlene was not about to emerge.

"Go downstairs in an hour. The hall porter will have an envelope with your name on it. The money will be there. Leave another envelope with Kristin's number for me. Mark it 'Mr. Smith.'"

"Okay," Junia had said. "Only don't you *dare* tell Darlene."

The deal had taken place on Saturday. Now with all this stuff going on about Hildie getting murdered and Mister X being involved and Kristin not coming home all night, Junia had the shakes. She wondered if she should confess to Darlene what she'd done.

No, she couldn't. She was too scared. Darlene had a vicious temper, and Junia didn't want to get thrown back onto the streets. She liked her setup. She even liked the dyke action, although that wasn't to say she was totally gay. Junia swung both ways, considering it prudent to keep one's options open.

Then she thought again about Kristin, whom she really liked because Kristin was a genuinely nice person, unlike Darlene's other girls, who were mostly stuck-up pieces of work Junia didn't get along with at all.

She could hear Darlene banging about in the bedroom. This was probably not a good time to tell her about Mister X's phone call, but Junia realized she'd better do something.

She ventured into the bedroom.

"Goddamn it!" Darlene screeched. "How *dare* the cunt drag me into this murder investigation. I'm suing her black ass right off television. You'll *never* see *her* again."

Darlene was on one of her rants. Once she got going there was no stopping her until she'd gotten satisfaction one way or another. Darlene, who presented a calm and sophisticated public image, was actually a raving bitch. However, over the eighteen months they'd been together, Junia had learned how to handle her moods.

"I am *not* happy," Darlene said ominously. "And I look like shit. I'm going to change." She stalked into her dressing room.

Junia hurried over to the notepad next to the phone. Darlene had a habit of writing everything down, and sure enough, there was the name of the guy she'd been talking to about Kristin—Jake Sica—and a number.

Junia didn't know what to do. It wasn't like she was a Good Samaritan or anything, but how could she sit back and do nothing? Hildie had been murdered, and indirectly it was probably Darlene's fault. She was sure Darlene didn't remember, but one night about six months ago she'd gotten drunk on a bottle of Cristal, and under the covers she'd confided to Junia the story of Kimberly and her connection to Mister X.

Junia had listened and said nothing. The next morning Darlene seemed completely oblivious to her ramblings of the previous night, and it was never mentioned again.

If Darlene went to jail, did that mean that she, Junia, would be left in the apartment with all the money and clothes and stuff?

Yes! She'd be the official custodian while Darlene was locked away. Wow! Not too bad a job.

Then reality hit. That's not the way it would work. No, she'd be thrown out quick as shit. She'd have nothing.

Surreptitiously she copied down Jake's phone number and slid it into the pocket of her jeans.

"Hey, Darl," she yelled through to the dressing room. "Want me to go to the cop station with you?"

"Are you *serious?*" Darlene said, marching back into the bedroom wearing a La Perla bronze lace slip on her well-toned body. "*You,* my dear, will stay out of this. Let us not forget where I found you. So I suggest for the next few weeks you keep a very low profile indeed. In fact, I don't even want you answering the phone. Let the service pick up."

"It's not like I have anybody calling me," Junia grumbled. "You don't allow me any friends."

"That's not fair," Darlene said sharply. "We live a different kind of lifestyle than other people. You're happy just to be with me, aren't you?"

Junia wanted to say, "No, you're twenty-three years older than me, and we've got nothing in common."

But she didn't. She knew she was living a cushy life, and she wasn't about to blow it.

At least not until she was good and ready.

chapter 14

THE FAMILY ENTERED FROM A
private room in the back and filed into the first pew.
They were led by the bereaved husband, Bobby
Skorch, who was heavily sedated or maybe stoned—
he could barely keep his balance. Bobby was clad in
an ankle-length black leather coat and dark shades;
his long, greasy, black hair was pulled back in a tight
ponytail. He was smoking a cigarette.

Behind him came Salli's father, a short stout man
with a carrot-color crew cut and a nervous tic. And
then followed two very young, fair-haired girls—
pretty in an unsophisticated way. They were Salli's
half sisters. Their mother, an overweight woman
wearing too much makeup and an unsuitable shiny
blue satin cocktail dress, trailed closely behind them.
And finally Grandpa, an old man with a wily gait,
wearing a shabby, ill-fitting brown suit.

Tucci's attention was on Bobby, the grieving husband, who'd been spotted last night picking up a girl on Sunset and taking her to a hotel. *Some grieving husband,* he thought. Hmm . . . he couldn't wait to hear Lee's report on the two strippers.

The more he thought about it, the more he was beginning to target Bobby Skorch as his prime suspect.

"That's Angela Musconni with Salli's ex," Cole said, nudging Madison.

She took a peek at the exquisite young woman who was walking in from the side door accompanied by a wild-looking guy with a mass of dirty blond hair. Salli had obviously harbored a penchant for guys who resembled out-of-control rock-'n'-rollers.

"So that's Eddie," Madison said in a low voice. "Salli talked about him on the tape, said he used to beat her."

"I told you that," Cole said. "Hadda make the hospital run a coupla times myself. In fact, Eddie and I duked it out one day."

"You did?"

"Yeah. I kinda got on him 'bout the way he was treatin' Salli, an' he called me a fag. So I beat the crap outta him." Cole laughed at the memory. "The dude deserved it. Treats women like shit."

"Do you think he could've murdered her?" Madison asked.

"Wouldn't surprise me."

She watched as Eddie and Angela sat down, noticing that as soon as they were settled, Angela began running her hands through the back of Eddie's hair and cooing in his ear. Obviously they were a couple.

Then Madison's attention was drawn to talk show host Bo Deacon, whom she'd met on the flight to L.A. It was only a few days ago, but it seemed like months had passed. Bo made a noisy entrance, demanding seats in front. He was with a zaftig redhead in her forties who clung to his arm as if she expected him to make a daring escape at any moment.

"Bo was coming on to Salli on the plane—or trying to," she whispered to Cole. "Only Salli wasn't buying his bullshit."

"Another slimeball," Cole said.

"You know everybody."

"In my job—sure. I'm kinda like a shrink or a barman—my clients spill the goods."

"You trained Bo?"

"For about three months. He's a lazy son of a bitch. Didn't wanna work it, then blamed me 'cause he continued to put on the pounds. So he fired me. *That* was the luckiest day of my life. He had hot and cold running women *and* a wife—a jealous wife."

"Charming."

"I used to work him out in his dressing room at the studio. There were all these little interns running in and out. His deal was to fuck 'em an' fire 'em."

Madison sighed. "Aren't there *any* nice guys in Hollywood?"

"Me."

"I mean nice *straight* guys."

"Hey—didn't you know?" Cole said with a big grin. "Straight guys are a dying breed."

"Thanks!"

"Why are we here?" Mrs. Bo Deacon demanded. Her name was Olive, and she was a former showgirl.

"Out of respect," Bo growled, wishing his wife would shut up. She was drunk as usual; he'd caught her slurping straight Scotch behind the bar at their house before they'd left for the funeral. "If I *wasn't* here, people would talk. Salli was on my show countless times."

I bet that wasn't all she was on, Olive thought with a hidden scowl. Did her cheating no-good husband think she didn't know what he was up to? If it wasn't for the children, and the glory of being married to a famous man, she would have left him years ago.

"I hope you don't expect me to go to the reception," Olive said, her overly glossed lips turning down at the corners. "Salli T. Turner was nothing more than a cheap tramp."

"How can you say that at her funeral for crissakes?" Bo objected, glancing around to make sure no one had heard.

"Because it's true," Olive hissed. "And I for one am not turning her into a saint now that she's dead."

"You're a real bitch, Olive," he said, getting a strong whiff of the Scotch on her breath.

"Yes, and don't you love it. *That's* why you married me."

No, he thought, *I married you because you had big tits and you were sexy as all get-out, and like a dumb schmuck I thought you'd stay that way.*

Unfortunately, now Olive was about as sexy as a sack of old beans. Plus she was a true lush, and however many times she promised him she'd stop drinking, it never happened. Two stays at the Betty Ford Clinic and it *still* didn't happen.

She muttered something to him. He wasn't listening; he was too busy waving at everyone in sight. He'd found, over the fifteen years that he and Olive had been married, that the only way to deal with her when she'd been drinking was to ignore her. Sometimes it actually worked.

By the time Natalie arrived in Westwood it was too late to get anywhere near the funeral. The crowds were huge. She located her camera crew and took up a position with them behind the ropes. The trick was to catch the celebrities on their way back to their cars. Some would speak to her. Some wouldn't. After all, this wasn't exactly a big movie premiere. This was a funeral—a hot funeral.

Natalie was on a high. Her story had gone over big; even Garth was pleased. This could be the start of a whole new direction for her, and it was about time. She was ready. She'd been ready since college.

The widower in the black leather coat leaned back on the hard wooden bench and let his tears flow as he listened to Mick Jagger screaming out "Satisfaction." He'd personally picked every track. They were not Salli's favorite songs, they were his. *He* was the one who'd been left behind. *He* was the goddamn survivor, so *he* could choose the music.

Nobody could see his tears, because his heavy black Ray-Bans concealed the action.

He swiped a hand across his cheeks, destroying any evidence of vulnerability. On the back of his hand there were two words tattooed through a blazing heart. *Salli Forever.*

And while Mick Jagger continued to yell out "Satisfaction," Bobby continued to wail his silent scream of unbearable pain.

chapter 15

STRUGGLING TO KEEP IT together, Kristin decided that lying on the floor and feeling sorry for herself was not going to help her situation. She was trapped—that much was obvious. She was naked, which made her even more vulnerable. And she was determined to survive this ordeal. She had to, for Cherie's sake.

She got up and took a long, deep breath. Then she went over to the small bed and frantically ripped off the one sheet. Holding it taut, she punched a hole in it with her fist, and then forced her head through the opening. Next she punched out two more holes for her arms and ripped off the bottom. Now she was wearing some kind of tentlike poncho, but at least she wasn't naked.

Next she inspected the wooden bed, dragging the sagging mattress onto the ground. The bed frame stood several inches off the floor, supported by four sturdy legs. Using all her strength she managed to tip the frame sideways. She inspected the legs closely. Yes! They screwed into the base. If she could dismantle the legs, she would have several formidable weapons to use on Mister X when he came back.

She needed a screwdriver—but where was she going to get *that*?

Easy. She still had her jewelry. A ring. Small stud earrings. A Saint Christopher medal that she never took off.

Unclasping the chain on her pendant, she worked with the small gold circle, slowly but surely loosening the first leg.

The feeling of triumph when it finally came off was intoxicating.

After a few minutes of rest, armed with the small but lethal weapon, she made a pass at the window, giving it a hearty whack. The glass shattered—which really got her adrenaline going, so much so that she hardly felt the shard of glass which cut across her arm. The pain meant nothing. Determination meant everything.

Brushing the broken glass out of her way, she went to work on the boards covering the window. Using the wooden leg as a battering ram, she attacked the middle board, using every ounce of strength she could muster. For a while she thought it wasn't going to give, but after half an hour of solid slamming, the board finally began to sag in the middle, causing her to strengthen her attack, even though she was dripping with perspiration and quite exhausted.

The small room was like a sweatbox with very little air. Outside she could hear the pounding of the ocean. Where was she? she wondered.

And where was Mister X?

What was his devious plan? Was it murder? Because if it was, he'd chosen the wrong victim.

chapter 16

THE FUNERAL SERVICE SEEMED
never-ending. Many people insisted on speaking, including Salli's agent, her manager, her publicist, her
female and male costars from the television series,
and finally her father—who mumbled a few almost
unintelligible words, so intense was his grief. Bobby
Skorch said nothing.

After the ceremony there was an air of frenzy.
Everyone was up and socializing. The crowds outside
were enormous, and as the celebrities filed out of the
chapel, screams from nearby fans filled the air. Three
or four helicopters hovered overhead, photographers
were balanced in trees with telephoto lenses, while the
cops went crazy trying to get everyone safely into
their cars and limos and out of there.

Madison stood outside with Cole, getting jostled on

all sides. "This is quite a scene," she commented, looking around in amazement.

"It sure is," Cole agreed. "And I want out."

That was easier said than done, though, since they were caught in human gridlock as everyone vied to get their cars first.

Somebody accidentally shoved Madison in the back. She turned around to object and came face-to-face with Bo Deacon. He looked at her as if he knew her, but couldn't quite remember from where.

"Mr. Deacon," she said. "Madison Castelli. Remember—we met on the plane a few days ago? You, me and Salli."

"What's that?" he said, attempting to back away, which was impossible because of the mass of people.

"On the plane, flying in from New York."

He moved backward, his wife moved forward. "I'm Mrs. Deacon," Olive announced coldly. "Who did you say you are, dear?"

"Madison Castelli. Your husband and I flew in from New York together. He wanted to sit next to Salli, so I changed seats. It's such a terrible tragedy, isn't it?"

Olive shot her husband a filthy look. "You wanted to sit next to Salli, huh?" she sneered as if she'd caught him jerking off in Times Square.

"For five minutes," Bo blustered. "I had some business to discuss with her."

"What kind of business?"

"Nothing important."

"You make me *sick.*"

"Be quiet, Olive," Bo said, desperately gesturing to

the valet. "Bring me my damn car at once. Don't you know who I am?"

Madison wondered what was going on with Bo and his wife. He appeared to be extremely agitated. And she was quite obviously drunk. A delightful couple.

Before she could wonder any further, Bobby emerged, surrounded by Salli's family. People fell back, making a path for him through the crowds. Salli's two little half sisters were crying, overcome with emotion. Their mother kept on urging them to be quiet.

"They shouldn't bring kids to something like this," Cole muttered. "Look at 'em, they're all confused. Probably never been out of Idaho before."

Salli's father was openly sobbing, tears rolling down his face.

A lone photographer managed to dart through security and started snapping pictures of the family.

Two guards leaped forward and grabbed him by the shoulder, smashing his camera to the ground. "You fuckers!" the photographer shouted. "I'm only doing my job."

Madison turned away in time to see Eddie Stoner pushing his way through the mob, dragging Angela Musconni behind him. Eddie was heading directly for Bobby, a purposeful look in his eye. "You did it, didn't you?" he yelled belligerently as he drew closer. "You . . . freakin' . . . did it."

Bobby refused to acknowledge him, but everyone else turned to gape unashamedly.

"C'mon—admit it! You motherfuckin' hypocrite," Eddie screeched. "You killed my Salli."

Bobby finally focused. "You talking to me?" he snapped. "You cowardly piece of dog shit."

"Yeah, it's *you* I'm talkin' to," Eddie responded, thrusting out his jaw.

The two little girls clung to their mother, terrified by the two angry men.

"Don't do this," Salli's father begged, tears streaming down his weathered cheeks. "Please don't make a scene."

"Make a scene?" Eddie shouted bitterly. "I'm gonna bash his freakin' face in."

Angie grabbed his arm. "Let's get out of here, Eddie," she urged. "This isn't doing you any good."

Eddie was on a roll. He shrugged her off, almost causing her to lose her balance. Then he threw a wild punch, cutting Bobby above the eye with his pinkie ring, and knocking off his dark glasses, which fell to the ground and shattered.

Bobby let out a roar of pain and fury and swung back. Before anyone could intervene, the two of them were embroiled in a vicious fistfight.

Paparazzi sprung out from everywhere, flashing away with their cameras, elbowing each other for the best position. The helicopters overhead hovered even lower. Several security guards leaped forward, intent on separating the two men—so intent that they forgot about controlling the media.

"Oh, God! I can't stand it. This is turning into a circus," Madison gasped.

"We'd better get our asses outta here," Cole responded, taking her by the arm. "We'll pick up the car later."

Half of her wanted to go, and the other half wanted to stay. There was a big story taking place right in front of her and she knew she had to cover it. "No," she said. "I have to see what happens."

"Somebody's gonna get hurt, that's what'll happen," Cole said, still attempting to pull her away.

Two of the guards had Eddie in a lock, with both his arms twisted behind him.

Bobby took the opportunity to smash his fist into Eddie's face. There followed the sound of teeth breaking and then blood began spurting.

"Leave him alone, you crazoid freak!" Angie screamed, jumping on Bobby and pummeling him with her fists. Bobby hauled back, shaking her off and then hitting her on the jaw. She dropped like a stone.

"Jesus!" Cole groaned. "Now I *gotta* get into it." And he went for Bobby, wrestling him to the ground.

Pandemonium reigned. Women were screaming. Men shouting and swearing. Like a swarm of mosquitoes the photographers were everywhere. And the TV news crews, sensing blood, broke ranks and added to the chaos.

In his struggle to get out of the way, Bo Deacon was accidentally hit in the face by a security guard. "My nose," he yelled. "You idiot! You've broken my fucking nose."

"Serves you right for coming here," Olive muttered.

"Get me to a fucking plastic surgeon," Bo screamed. "And shut the fuck up!"

There was not enough security to control what was

going on. The entire aftermath of the funeral was turning into some kind of crazed celebrity riot.

And there was absolutely nothing anyone could do.

By the time Tucci made it to the scene, everybody was involved. Quickly taking in the situation, he shoved his way through the crowds, grabbing Cole off Bobby—who now had a bloody nose as well as a gash over his left eye. Tucci summoned the help of a couple of cops.

Angie staggered to her feet. "I want that man arrested!" she screamed, pointing an accusing finger at Bobby. "The prick assaulted me. I want him arrested."

"Go fuck yourself, cunt!" Bobby responded.

"You *dumb* asshole!" Angie screamed. "Look what you've done to Eddie. Look at him!"

Eddie could hardly talk. He was sitting on the ground with blood gushing from his mouth; two of his front teeth were missing.

Tucci took control of the situation. "You'd all better come to the station," he said. "We'll sort it out there."

"You bet!" Angie yelled, pointing at Bobby. "I'm suing his ass! We're pressing charges."

Meanwhile the cameras captured every exquisite, celebrity moment.

chapter 17

"**A**RE YOU JAKE?" JUNIA said.

"Who wants to know?" Jake asked, cradling the phone.

"You interested in hearing about Kristin?"

"Where is she?" he asked, jumping to attention.

"You got money?"

"What is this—a shakedown?"

"I know stuff about Kristin you'll want to hear. But I gotta get paid for my information, 'cause if I give it up, I'll have to scoot outta town."

"How *much* money?"

"How much you got?"

"This conversation is dumb—I don't even know who you are."

"Your girlfriend could be in danger."

x

81

"What kind of danger?"

"You read about that blonde found dead in the ocean? It could've been Kristin."

"Who *are* you?"

"If you've got ten thousand dollars, we can meet. If you don't, forget it."

"Where am *I* going to come up with ten thousand dollars?"

"Not my problem."

"You sound like a crazy person."

"Insults make me want to hang up."

"Okay, okay, I'll meet you," he said, deciding that the smart thing to do was to find out what this was about. After all, if Kristin was in trouble, he wanted to help.

"And you'll bring cash?"

"Yes," he lied impatiently. "Where do we meet?"

"There's a restaurant, Chin Chin, on Sunset Plaza. I'll be at a table outside. Be there in an hour."

"How will I know you?"

"I'm wearing an orange sweater. And don't blow it—if you want Kristin safe, you'd better bring the money."

Jake put down the phone, his mind in turmoil. What in hell was going on here? And what could *he* do?

First of all, he'd hardly brought any money to L.A. with him—six or seven hundred dollars at the most. His bank was in Arizona, and there was no way he could make a withdrawal that size today. And who was the mystery person on the phone? It certainly wasn't the woman who'd called Kristin's answering machine—this woman sounded much younger.

Quickly realizing he needed help, he picked up the

phone and called his brother at the TV station. Jimmy wasn't there, so he tried him at home and got his wife.

"Jakie—we miss you," Bunny cooed. "When are you coming to dinner again?" She'd obviously forgotten the petulant fit she'd thrown the last time he was there.

"Tell Jimmy to call me as soon as possible," he said, hanging up and pacing furiously around the room.

What next? he wondered. Suddenly he thought of Madison. She was an intelligent woman and a journalist. She was also the only friend he had in L.A. Hoping that she'd have some ideas, he called her.

"Hi, Jake," Madison said breathlessly. "I just walked in. You're not going to *believe* what happened at Salli's funeral. Put on your TV, I'm sure it'll be all over the four-o'clock news."

"There's something urgent I have to discuss with you," he said. "Can I come by?"

"Of course."

"See you in a minute," he said, grabbing his leather jacket and racing downstairs, stopping at the desk to tell them where he'd be. Then he jumped in his truck and drove over.

Madison greeted him at the door. "You sounded like it's something important."

"It is," he said grimly.

"Come in and tell me everything. You remember Cole, don't you?"

"Yeah—hi, Cole," he said. "Uh . . . Madison, this is kind of private. Can we talk somewhere quiet?"

"Hey, man, you caught me on my way out," Cole said. "I got appointments backed up, an' they're all gettin' pissed at me, 'cause since *this* lady hit town I never get anythin' done. It's more of a kick hangin' with her."

"Didn't mean to be rude," Jake said.

"No sweat," Cole said, kissing Madison on the cheek. "She'll tell you all about our insane funeral experience. It's a story, man."

"Can I get you anything to drink?" Madison asked as soon as Cole left. "Seven-Up? Evian? Pellegrino? We've got it all."

He shook his head and sat down. Madison looked great as usual, and she seemed to be free of complications. Why couldn't he have met *her* first? "Remember I told you about a woman I was seeing?"

"Kristin, wasn't that her name?"

"Yeah, well . . . I did what you suggested and tried calling her. She wasn't there, and, according to her maid, she didn't come home last night. Which I guess, considering the business she's in, is not unusual. However, she *still* hasn't gotten home, and a short while ago I got a weird call from some girl who informs me Kristin's in danger, and if I meet her and hand over ten thousand bucks, she'll fill me in."

"You're kidding?"

He shrugged. "No, although I thought *she* was. That's exactly how I felt. I mean I know L.A.'s got a crazy reputation, but this has to be a bad joke, right?"

"Let me get this straight," Madison said, frowning. "Kristin didn't come home last night. You haven't spoken since you walked out on her. Now you've got this person calling, demanding money."

"That's about it. She mumbled something about a dead blonde in the ocean."

"Oh, God!"

"What?"

"Did you happen to watch Natalie on the news today?"

"No."

"She had a story on the blonde. She was a call girl—worked for a madam called Darlene. Does that name mean anything to you?"

"Darlene? No."

"Wait a minute," Madison said, thinking fast. "Do you have Kristin's number?"

"Yeah."

"Give it to me, I've got an idea."

"Hey, listen, we don't have time. I'm supposed to meet my mystery caller at Chin Chin in an hour—which," he said, glancing at his watch, "is now in about half an hour."

"Let me try this first," Madison said, punching out the number. Chiew answered the phone. "I'm looking for Kristin," Madison said.

"Madam not here," Chiew said.

"Is she at Darlene's?"

"No," Chiew said. "Don't know where."

"Damn!" Madison said. "I owe her money. What's Darlene's number? I'm in my car and don't have it with me."

Chiew gave her the number.

Madison hung up. "I want you to take a look at something," she said to Jake.

"I gotta get going," he said impatiently.

Madison pushed Natalie's videotape into the VCR and began playing it for him. "I think Darlene could

85

be your girlfriend's madam, too," she said. "And I have a feeling that whoever you're supposed to meet is right. Kristin might be in trouble."

"Shit!"

Madison jumped up. "C'mon, Jake," she said firmly. "I'll go with you. Between us, we'll find out exactly what's going on."

chapter 18

LATER IN THE DAY, WHEN Max showed definite signs of improvement, Diana had him moved out of intensive care and into a private suite. He was conscious and well aware of the fact that she was sitting beside him, holding his hand.

"How are you feeling?" she asked anxiously.

"Like I had a battle with a rhinoceros," he groaned. "What happened to me?"

"You got shot."

"Shot?" he said, managing a laugh. "Who did it—a dissatisfied actress?"

"The police would like you to try and identify some mug shots when you're ready."

He sighed. "Oh, yeah, yeah, I *really* feel like doin' that. Y'know, identify some gang member who's gonna come back and cream my ass. I think not." He struggled to sit up, wincing with pain. "Hey, how come *you're* here?"

"I came as soon as I heard. I stayed with you all night."

"That's nice of you."

"It's more than nice, Max. I think you must know how I—"

Before she could finish her sentence, the door opened and Freddie strode in. "Well," Freddie said. "What kind of a situation did you get yourself into this time?"

"I've done worse, haven't I?" Max said, grinning weakly.

Freddie gave a dry laugh. "A lot worse. The good thing is that you're okay. Has Diana been looking after you?"

"She's the best," Max said. "Thanks for the loan."

"With my compliments," Freddie said, infuriating Diana.

An attractive black nurse entered the room. "Everything all right, Mr. Steele?"

"Perfect."

"Ring if you need me."

"Not bad," Max said as the pretty nurse retreated.

"Congratulations," Freddie said. "Diana told me you're engaged. Who's the unlucky lady?"

Max struggled to figure out what Freddie was talking about, then it started to come back to him. Kristin. Hadn't he told her to come to his house? Oh God, was she going to laugh when she heard *this* one. Maybe an engagement wasn't such a good idea after all, although it might stop Diana, who had been about to say something intimate when Freddie arrived. Yes, he'd be wise to keep the story going. "I'm engaged to a beautiful girl called Kristin," he said. "You haven't met her, but you will."

"Where is she?" Freddie said, turning to Diana with a questioning expression.

"I tried calling her," Diana explained. "The phone was answered by a woman called Darlene who was extremely rude."

Max knew exactly what must have happened— Diana had connected with Kristin's madam. He choked back a laugh. Thank God she hadn't put it together. "Oh, yeah," he mumbled. "Darlene's her cousin. Sometimes she stays there."

"Give me Kristin's number and I'll phone her personally," Freddie said. "Can't wait to see the woman who's hooked *you.*"

"Don't want to worry her," Max said.

"She must be worried anyway," Freddie said. "Not hearing from you."

"To tell you the truth," Max lied, "she was so happy we got engaged that she went to visit her family in San Diego. I guess that's why you couldn't reach her, Diana. She'll be back in a few days, so let's not worry her for now."

"If that's the way you want it," Freddie said.

"That's the way . . ." Max said, feeling sleep creeping up on him.

"Is there anything I can do?" Freddie asked.

"Yeah," Max said, grimacing. "Tell me all is forgiven. I was a schmuck."

"I think we've both realized we're a team," Freddie said gravely. "I'm taking the rest of the day off. If you need anything, Ria can reach me."

"Where are you going?" Diana asked.

"I need to be alone for a while," Freddie said. "I'm driving to the beach house."

"What time will you be home?"

"Maybe I'll stay overnight," he said abruptly. "I'll call you later."

"Whyn't you take Diana with you?" Max mumbled. "I'm sure there's a bunch of gorgeous nurses on call, an' your wife's been here all night."

"No," Diana said stubbornly. "I want to stay."

"You look tired, Diana," Freddie said. "Max is well taken care of. I'll drop you at home."

Diana realized this was neither the time nor the place to take a stand. First she'd better deal with the fiancée situation; then, when Max was out of the hospital, they could talk about their future together. "Very well," she said, deeply disappointed. "I'll come back later if you like, Max."

"Don't like," he slurred, almost out. "You've been great, but, please, I gotta sleep."

"Then I'll be here first thing in the morning."

"Whatever."

"Can I bring you anything?"

"Yeah, a stack of *Playboy*s to cheer me up." Her mouth slid into a tight, disapproving line. "Only kidding," he said. "What's the problem? You don't approve of *Playboy?*"

"The name says it all," Diana said primly. "You're not a boy and you don't play."

"C'mon," Max said. "Lighten up." He gave them both a weak wave, waited until they were out of the room, then rang for the nurse and requested a phone.

"You're not allowed any calls, Mr. Steele," the

nurse said. "Don't forget, you're only just out of intensive care. Rest and sleep—that's all you're supposed to do."

"Anybody ever told you you've got a great—" He yawned and settled back on the pillow. "Nah—forget it."

"A great what, Mr. Steele?"

"I'm changing my ways," he mumbled, and fell into a deep sleep.

chapter 19

LEE ECCLES STOPPED TUCCI as soon as he entered the station. "What in hell's going on?" he asked, falling into step beside him.

"Big brawl at the funeral," Tucci said, hitching up his pants. "I've got 'em all coming in. Everyone wants to press charges."

"Who're you talkin' about?"

"Bobby Skorch, Eddie Stoner—those are the only two that matter. If we move fast, we can throw a few questions at 'em before their lawyers arrive."

"Got it," Lee said. "Let *me* take Bobby."

"What's the story with the strippers?"

"They flew in with him, he checked 'em into a hotel, then he split a coupla times—which gives him the opportunity. As an alibi they're less than zero."

"The more I see him, the more I think he could've

done it," Tucci said. "I got a blood sample—one from Eddie, too."

"How'd you manage that?"

"They're both bleeding. I did a little mopping up with my handkerchief and jacket. Bobby's the handkerchief, Eddie's the jacket. Faye'll kill me when she sees I've ruined her favorite jacket."

"Oh yeah, Faye," Lee said with a knowing smirk. "Mustn't piss *her* off."

Tucci shot him a look. He didn't want to hear Faye's name coming out of Lee's mouth. If there wasn't so much going on he would've gotten into exactly what Lee meant every time he mentioned his wife.

As it was, there was no time for anything. Eddie and Angie came rolling into the station, Angie still screaming about assault charges. They were followed closely by Bobby, who wanted Eddie arrested. And then came Bo Deacon with his wife.

Trailing closely behind them were hordes of media, but they had to stay outside, jockeying for position, waiting for when the principals emerged.

Captain Marsh poked his head out of his office. "What in *hell* is going on here?" he demanded.

It was at that exact moment that Darlene and her lawyer chose to arrive.

"Why'd you do it, Bobby?"

Slouched on a chair in the interview room, determined to get Eddie Stoner's ass slung in jail, upset from the funeral, depressed and suicidal about Salli, Bobby Skorch stared blankly at the tall, stoop-shouldered detective with the weather-beaten face and exceptionally large hands.

"What?" he said, his eyes blank and red-rimmed, with no shades to hide his pain or his worsening black eye from the world.

"Why'd you kill her?" Lee Eccles demanded, leaning over the table and eyeballing Bobby with a ferocious glare.

Bobby's head snapped back. "Who the fuck d'you think you're *talkin'* to?" he said in a low, angry voice. "What the fuck is *this* shit?"

"Your two little scum-buckets from Vegas blew your alibi out the window," Lee said, scrambling for a used toothpick in his jacket pocket.

"Hey—" Bobby said, reality hitting home through his conflicted haze of self-hatred and drug-induced euphoria. "Get me my fucking lawyer."

"Your fucking lawyer ain't here," Lee said, not trying to hide his loathing for the famous person sitting before him. Loathing him because he had everything Lee didn't—including a sex-symbol wife who any red-blooded American male would give his left ball to fuck. *Excuse me,* Lee thought, angrily chewing on his newly found toothpick. *Dead wife. Murdered wife. Hacked-to-pieces wife.*

"You're outta line," Bobby said harshly. "I came here to straighten out a situation. You can't accuse me of shit."

"I'm only askin', Bobby. Thought you might wanna make a confession."

"Go fuck yourself in the ass. You wanna know who killed Salli? It was Eddie Stoner, an' you got him here now—so do somethin' about it."

"Where *did* you go Saturday night when you got

back? Didja go to your house an' catch Salli with another guy? Was that what happened?"

"Jesus!" Bobby screamed. "Don't you understand English? *Eddie Stoner murdered my wife,* and I want him in jail. Got it, moron?"

Oblivious to the scene going on in the next room, Tucci was attempting to calm Angela Musconni. Eddie Stoner slumped in a chair beside her, clutching a blood-soaked wad of Kleenex to his mouth. It was almost as if he'd lost his balls along with his two front teeth.

Angie, however, more than made up for his silence. She was acting like a wildcat, jumping up and down, pummeling the air with her fists to get her point across. "You gotta arrest the prick," she yelled. "Eddie said Bobby did it, an' Eddie knows what he's talkin' about. An' if you *can't* arrest him for the murder, you can sure as crap arrest him for personal assault. He knocked Eddie's *teeth* out and hit me too. I was lying on the ground *unconscious!* I'm pressin' charges. Arrest the prick! I demand it!"

"If we arrest him, Miss Musconni," Tucci said candidly, "it won't look good for you *or* us. The man was leaving his wife's funeral. He was provoked into a fight. There are dozens of witnesses who saw exactly what took place. His lawyer will bail him immediately, and then there'll be a long, drawn-out court battle with all the attendant publicity. Are you sure you want that?"

"No!" Eddie managed to say, spitting out more blood.

"Yes!" Angie insisted.

Tucci regarded the two of them, trying to decide who had the power in the relationship. Right now it was probably Angie—she was certainly the more vocal. But if she pressed charges against Bobby at this particular moment, it would complicate things. When the time came, they'd nail Bobby Skorch, but it would be for murder, not this petty stuff.

"Can I be frank with you both?" Tucci said. "Can I trust you?"

"Huh?" Angie said, suspicion narrowing her eyes.

"Mr. Skorch is indeed a suspect in the murder of Salli T. Turner, so an arrest at this time for assault would do nothing but hamper our investigation."

"Why?" Angie demanded.

"Because if we arrest him on a minor charge, it would not help us." He watched her carefully; she seemed to be listening, which was a good thing. "This is what I'd like you to do," he said.

"What?"

"I'd like you to go home, think about it, and if you still wish to press charges you can do so tomorrow. Is that fair?"

Eddie nodded vigorously. Angie was still not convinced.

"Miss Musconni," Tucci said in his most persuasive voice. "Do the smart thing. I promise, you won't regret it."

"Get me to a plastic surgeon," Bo Deacon whimpered as Olive drove their Rolls erratically down Wilshire Boulevard.

"I'm taking you to the emergency room," Olive

said, not at all upset at her famous husband's predicament.

"Don't wanna go to emergency," he groaned. "I want a plastic surgeon."

"Shame your little sweetie is dead," Olive said, weaving erratically from one lane to the other. "I'm sure she was an expert when it comes to plastic surgeons. Let's see, she had silicone tits, pumped-up lips, false cheekbones, a new chin—probably a brand-new pussy after all the action the old one got."

"Jesus, you're a bitch," Bo said, wishing he was anywhere else. "She was twenty-two years old for God's sake. And she's dead."

"Good," Olive said.

"Good?" Bo repeated, not quite able to believe she'd said such a thing.

"Did you fuck her?" Olive inquired, tossing back her red hair.

"What?"

"Did you?"

"You're crazy," he said, disgusted.

"Did you do her on the plane, Bo Bo, did you?"

"Jesus, Olive, I can't even talk to you anymore."

"You went to her house, I know you did."

"Are you *insane?*"

"Oh, yes. Saturday. You were there, sniffing around while her husband was away."

"You've lost it."

"Have I?"

"I'm in pain."

"I don't care," she said with a drunken smile, nearly smashing his precious Rolls into the back of a truck.

"You're drunk," he said, stating the obvious. "Stop the car and let me drive."

"I'm drunk," she singsonged. "And you've been fucking around on me. Who's the baddest, Bo Bo?"

"Come on, Olive, not now."

"When?" she demanded, taking her eyes off the road and giving him a long, pained look. "When's *my* time?"

"My nose is broken!" he screamed. "I'm warning you, Olive, don't get into this now!"

"I hate you!" she bellowed, her face contorted with drunken fury as she hit the gas even harder. "Hate you! Hate you! Hate you!"

"For God's sake, Olive!"

And before he could do anything to stop her, she swung the wheel of the powerful car toward the oncoming traffic, and smashed head-on into a gold Mercedes.

chapter 20

IT HAD TAKEN HER HOURS, BUT Kristin had finally managed to remove the middle board in the window. Unfortunately the space was only four inches high and two feet across, not big enough for her to squeeze through, but at least she could get some idea of where she was. As far as she could tell she was in some kind of guardhouse halfway down a cliff. The undergrowth on the cliff was unkempt and wild, which made her think that nobody ever came to this building. Several hundred feet below her was the ocean, and there seemed to be no other properties in sight.

She'd tried desperately to pry the rest of the window boards loose, but after a while she'd given up. It was impossible. Her hands were cut and bleeding, and there was a gash on her arm. She was lucky to have gotten the middle board out of there without breaking a bone.

Being able to look out and get some idea of where she was struck her as a major triumph.

What she couldn't figure out was *why* she'd allowed herself to be led down a dangerous cliffside blindfolded. She must have been crazy. One false step and she could've fallen hundreds of feet to her death.

Little lamb goes quietly to the slaughter.

What kind of a monster was Mister X anyway? she asked herself. Did he get a sexual kick out of this? Whatever. Clearly his motives were evil. *He* was evil.

The good thing was that she no longer felt like a victim. She had a plan and a weapon, and even though she was hungry and thirsty, she was determined to remain strong.

Now that she had some light, she could explore the room properly. Not that there was much to explore— bare floorboards, the bed, one sheet that she was now wearing, and nothing else.

She'd thought long and hard about what she would do if and when Mister X returned, and she'd finally decided her only move was to take him by surprise, try to knock him out, and escape. If she could do that and make it to the highway, she'd be able to summon help.

The thought of Cherie depending on her gave her strength.

Her inner voice had stopped screaming vile things in her head. Now it urged her to be strong.

Don't be frightened. You can do it. You're a survivor.

Yes. She was. And she *would* survive.

Of that she was sure.

chapter 21

"**T**HAT'S HER," MADISON said, striding confidently toward the open-air restaurant.

"How do you know?" Jake said, squinting at the fair-haired girl sitting at a table by herself leafing through a copy of *Movieline*.

"One, she's alone. Two, she's wearing an orange sweater. Pretty easy to be smart under these circumstances. Did you get her name?"

"Nope."

"Well, okay, let's go over."

Jake put his hand on her arm, stopping her. "She's expecting me to be by myself. She's also expecting ten grand, which I don't have."

"We'll suss the situation out," Madison said. "Let *me* do the talking."

He wasn't sure if he liked Madison's new take-charge attitude. "You can be incredibly bossy," he remarked.

"You wanted help, didn't you?" she fired back. "Come on, let's do it."

Together they approached the girl in the orange sweater. She was busy reading an article on Vince Vaughn, and did not look up until Madison said, "Hi."

"Yes?" Junia said, her eyes darting this way and that.

"Meet Jake Sica," Madison said. "I'm his sister."

"Sister?"

"We're twins. We do everything together."

Junia wrinkled her forehead. What kind of a kinky scene was *this?* "Where's my money?" she said, putting down the magazine.

"Safe," Madison said matter-of-factly. "But of course, as I'm sure you're aware, we can't hand it over without knowing what we're paying for."

"I *told* him to bring the money," Junia said, slamming her delicate fist on the table.

"He did," Madison said calmly, pulling out a chair and sitting down—gesturing for Jake to do the same. "Here's the deal. Why settle for ten grand when you can make a lot more?"

"How?" Junia asked suspiciously.

"Did you ever hear of Watergate?"

"What's that, a bridge?"

"No. Watergate was an event in history. People with the right information made plenty of money out of Watergate."

"I don't get it," Junia said, intrigued in spite of herself, and starting to feel quite important.

"Do you work for Darlene?" Madison asked, thinking that this waif of a girl was the least likely looking call girl she'd ever seen.

"Work for her?" Junia snorted as if it was the most ridiculous thing she'd ever heard. "No way! S'matter of fact, I live with her." As soon as she'd said it, she regretted her words. She wasn't supposed to tell them anything about *her*. No way. Her plan was to get the money and take off.

"You mean you're her girlfriend?"

"S' right," Junia said, nodding vigorously.

"Platonic or otherwise?"

"What d'*you* think?" Junia said with a sly smile.

"Where's Kristin?" Jake said, getting impatient.

Junia ignored him, more interested in what the woman had to say. "What do you mean I can make more money?" she questioned.

"I'm sure you have a very interesting story to tell," Madison said. "And if you're prepared to reveal details about Darlene and exactly how she runs her business, well, I think we could be talking about a *lot* of money."

Junia's eyes popped. "A lotta money, huh?"

"Right," Madison continued, silencing Jake with a warning look. "I work for *Manhattan Style* magazine. If you agree to give us an exclusive, I'm sure I can get my editor to pay you twenty thousand dollars."

"Wow!" Junia exclaimed reverently.

"Here's my card," Madison said, fishing in her purse.

Junia took the engraved card and studied it. "How do I know this isn't a fake?" she asked.

"Why would I go to that kind of trouble?" Madison

replied. "You see, we've been planning on writing an exposé on the call-girl industry for quite some time. My brother Jake's a photographer, that's his involvement. He was about to take some photos of Kristin for the magazine."

"Was she cooperating with you?" Junia asked.

"She certainly was," Jake said, getting Madison's drift and joining in. "Which is why it's so disturbing that she's vanished."

"I'm glad you're smart enough to get out now, while you can," Madison said, speaking fast. "We can put you in a hotel for your own protection. I'll have a contract from the magazine FedExed here immediately. Only thing is—you *have* to tell us how to find Kristin."

"Dunno where she is," Junia said. "But I do know that Mister X got her home number, and *he's* the client who had a date with Hildie. And . . ." She stopped, realizing she might be saying too much. "There's more about him, but I need t' see money first."

"Who's Mister X?" Jake asked with a distinct note of urgency.

Junia shrugged. "Nobody knows, not even Darlene. He calls every so often, whenever he wants a girl."

"The phone company," Jake said. "If he called Kristin, maybe they'll have a record of his number."

"I don't think it works that way," Madison said.

"We can give it a shot. It's better than doing nothing."

Madison turned to Junia. "Listen," she said. "You shouldn't go home. We'll check you into a hotel, all expenses paid."

"Why *can't* I go home?" Junia whined. "Darlene doesn't know I'm meeting you."

"Darlene's in trouble," Madison said. "She's all over the TV. You'll be better off in hiding until we get your story. And remember, it's exclusive, or no big check."

"Well, okay," Junia said reluctantly. "But I'd better get paid tomorrow, otherwise the deal's off."

"Done," Madison said.

There was nothing that excited her more than a hot story. And she could tell this was going to be a good one.

chapter 22

"I'VE BEEN KEPT WAITING for forty-five minutes," Darlene said, although Linden had warned her it was not smart to complain. "Forty-five minutes," she repeated icily, not particularly caring whether it was smart or not.

"Sorry, ma'am," Tucci said politely, sitting down across from the well-groomed, extremely attractive woman and her Beverly Hills lawyer. "Emergency situation arose."

"I was forced to rush my lunch to be here on time," Darlene said, pushing her point home.

Christ! *She* was complaining. All *he'd* had to eat all day was three lousy donuts, and the way things were going he'd be working straight through dinner. Hopefully Faye would save him something. Lately he'd been daydreaming about her pot roast. The good thing was that over the last few days he must have lost at least ten pounds. Goodbye diet. Hello food.

"We understand you have some questions you'd like to ask Ms. La Porte," Linden said. "Can we kindly proceed."

"Certainly," Tucci said. It had taken him a while, but he'd finally convinced Angela Musconni not to press charges against Bobby Skorch. She'd left with Eddie—reluctantly.

Meanwhile, Lee had managed to upset Bobby, who'd stalked out of the station just as his lawyer arrived. Marty Steiner was not a happy camper, furious that they'd had Bobby to themselves for an hour. Marty would be even more furious if he knew that even now the lab was running blood-sample tests which could possibly connect his client to Salli's murder.

Tucci was in no mood to conduct an interview with some Hollywood madam, who probably had more connections than a multi-purpose vacuum. He knew the way these things worked. These women always had clients in high places who eventually put on the pressure to get the charges dropped. Not that they had anything to charge Darlene La Porte with. She was a known madam, but right now they had no concrete proof. Her girls wouldn't talk, nor would her rich and famous clients. To nail Darlene they'd have to put some kind of entrapment plan in the works. And now was not the time.

"We appreciate you coming in," Tucci said.

"Appreciate away," Darlene said, shooting him a haughty look. "The sooner I'm out of here, the better."

"Yes, ma'am."

"And *don't* call me ma'am."

Madison was on a roll. In her mind she visualized the story she was going to write about L.A. and it had her adrenaline pumping. For the time being she forgot about Freddie Leon, because right now she was into investigating the call-girl business. It had all the ingredients for a killer story. Power. Obsession. Murder. Revenge. Her kind of deal.

And Junia—Darlene La Porte's almost underage lesbian lover—was set to spill everything.

They'd stashed Junia in a room in Jake's hotel, made sure she had Spectravision and room service; then they'd gone to Jake's room, where Madison sat on his bed and called Victor in New York.

"Have I got a story for you!" she bragged.

"Freddie Leon was *that* interesting?" Victor boomed in his annoyingly loud voice.

"Not Freddie," she said excitedly. "Bigger and better. Only you've got to come up with a check for twenty grand pronto."

"Excuse me?"

"I have a songbird from the inside of an exclusive call-girl operation. And she's ready to Whitney Houston it."

"You know, sometimes I don't understand a word you say."

"That's okay," she said breezily. "Make the check out to cash and FedEx it to me at once. We'll have a story that'll blow the magazine off the stands."

"Now wait a minute—"

"No waiting, Victor. And I want to work with a

great photographer who just *might* be available." She winked at Jake, who couldn't believe this was the same Madison he'd gotten used to. "He's expensive, but you should definitely consider signing him. His name's Jake Sica. I'll let you know if we can get him."

"Madison—"

"Bye, Victor." She hung up and turned to Jake. "Why work for some popular crap mag when I can get you a gig on *Manhattan Style?*"

"What happened to you?" he said, shaking his head at her metamorphosis. "You're all fired up."

She beamed. "I feel good. In fact, I feel *great*. I'm back in action. This story's going to be *sensational*. Let's go tell Junia the good news."

"I need to find Kristin," he said. "That's the only important thing to me."

For a moment she felt a shiver of disappointment. Just when she'd thought she and Jake were a great team . . .

"Sorry," she said quickly. "You're right, and I have an idea."

"What?"

"We should go by her apartment, see what we can find."

"The maid'll never let us in."

"Jake," she bragged. "Doncha know? You're working with *me* now, and when I'm into it, *I* can do anything."

chapter 23

PROPPED UP IN BED, WATCH-
ing the unbelievable goings-on at Salli T. Turner's
funeral on the TV news, Max Steele was completely
comfortable and out of pain thanks to the miracle of
modern drugs. The nurses were all fans. Well, how
often was it that they got their hands on a genuine
eligible Bel Air bachelor? They kept on popping into
his room, two at a time, to take a peek at him and ask
a question or two, such as did he know Matt Damon?
And was Anne Heche really gay or was she just going
with Ellen for the publicity? Normal questions the
general public liked to ask.

Max got off on being the center of attention. He had
his eye on the pretty black nurse—she had a Halle
Berry quality about her, and he liked her personality,
not to mention her perky tits.

Yes, all in all, it wasn't *that* bad getting shot, and

110

now Freddie wasn't mad at him anymore, which was a good thing, and as soon as he recovered and recuperated at say—the Four Seasons in Maui—it would be back to business as usual.

He kept on drifting in and out of sleep, which was quite pleasant. *Gotta call Kristin,* he thought. *She must've wondered what happened to me. Gotta call her . . .*

Boom. His eyes closed. He was asleep again, which is how Inga Cruelle and Howie Powers found him when they burst into his room.

"Jesus, man," Howie exclaimed, waking him up. "You frightened the shit outta us."

Us? Did that mean the delectable Inga and his erstwhile friend—the brain-dead playboy—were an us?

"How'd you find out?" he mumbled.

"Your maid told me when I dropped by your house," Howie said, picking at a bunch of grapes on the bedstand. "What a bummer!"

"When was that?"

"'Bout an hour ago, soon as we got back from Vegas."

"Didja win?"

Howie beamed, and put his arm around Inga's waist, pulling the exquisite Swedish supermodel close. "I won the prize of all time. Inga did me the honor of becoming my wife."

"Whaaat?" Max tried to sit up, but sharp stabs of pain prevented him from doing so. "You got *married?*"

Inga gave a supermodel sneer—the one she'd perfected on runways all over the world. "That is right, Max dear. Howard and I are joined in matrimony."

Max could not believe what he was hearing. Howie Powers and Inga Cruelle married? Impossible. He, Max Steele, hadn't even fucked her, and she'd married a major jerk like Howie. What was going on in the world? This was insanity.

"Show him the ring, honey," Howie urged.

Inga waved her hand under his nose. On her engagement finger was an enormous diamond, at least ten carats.

"Congratulations," Max managed, the words almost sticking in his throat. "What happened to your fiancé, Inga? The Swedish guy you told me you've been with since high school?"

She shrugged. "Howie is very sweet," she said. "And persuasive. He came to see me last night at midnight. So touching."

"With the ring?"

"Naturally."

"Yup," Howie said happily. "I got to thinkin', I've been a bachelor long enough. We flew to Vegas this morning, did it, and the first person we came to tell was you, 'cause you're my best friend, buddy."

Yeah, sure, Max thought. *You came to show me your prize. Because for once in your life, you rich little asshole, you got a girl before me. Well, good luck, 'cause this one's gonna take you for a lot more than a diamond ring. And you're such a schmuck, I bet you never had her sign a pre-nup.*

"I couldn't be happier for you," Max said, full of insincerity.

"Howard," Inga said, glancing at her Patek Phillipe

diamond watch—a wedding present Howie had presented to her on the flight home. "I have to go."

"Gotta get my bride to the airport," Howie said. "She's off to Milan for the collections."

"*You're* not going?"

"Havta take care of some business first. I'll join her in a coupla days."

As if Howie, the playboy jerk, had any business to take care of. All Howie did was watch his trust funds grow, that was about it.

"Well . . ." Max said. "Thanks for dropping by."

"Your turn next," Howie said, winking.

Ha! Max thought. *Wait until he sees Kristin. She makes Inga look like a skinny version of truly gorgeous. No contest.*

"I'll see you guys," he said.

Inga blew him a kiss. Nice of her. Howie winked again and mouthed, "Somethin', huh?"

And then they were gone.

Max waited a minute and summoned Halle Berry. Life wasn't all that bad.

chapter 24

TUCCI WAS SITTING AT HIS desk when he got the call that Bo Deacon had been killed in a horrendous car accident on Wilshire. His wife, Olive, who had been driving at the time, had been rushed to Cedars with multiple cuts and bruises, but nothing life-threatening.

She was conscious, hysterical and insisting on seeing one of the detectives in charge of the Salli T. Turner murder investigation.

Since Lee had gone off to re-interview several of Salli's neighbors, Tucci guessed he was it. What a day this was turning out to be. Bo Deacon killed in a car wreck. Talk about bad karma. You leave a funeral and run right into your own death.

Fate. The twists and turns of life. Never predictable.

Tucci left the station and drove to the hospital,

calling Faye from the car. "Do you miss me?" he asked wistfully.

"Yes, I miss you," she answered. "When will you be home?"

"Not soon enough."

"How was the funeral?"

"Hectic. Did you see the news?"

"I'll turn it on."

"Faye?"

"Yes."

"I don't want to do this diet thing anymore."

"Why?"

"Life's too short." A beat. "Are we too old to have a baby instead?"

She laughed softly. "What's a baby got to do with dieting?"

"Thought we could get fat together."

"Yes."

"Yes?"

"Yes."

"I love you. Can I have pot roast for dinner?"

"You can have anything you want."

By the time he reached the hospital he had a big smile on his face. Sometimes it was nice to goof off, have nonsensical conversations, fall in love with his wife all over again.

There was a uniformed cop stationed outside Olive Deacon's room. "What's going on?" Tucci asked.

The cop spoke out of the side of his mouth like he didn't want anyone to hear. "She's hysterical, Detective, and drunk."

"So?"

"So she's confessing to Salli Turner's murder."

"Hi," said Madison, standing at Kristin's front door. "I spoke with Kristin and she asked me to tell you that she'll be home shortly."

Chiew, Kristin's maid, stared at her blankly, guarding the entrance to her boss's apartment with her sturdy body.

"She also asked me to wait for her here, but if you're not comfortable with me coming inside . . ." Madison shrugged, as if it didn't matter one way or the other.

Chiew stared at her for a few more seconds, and then decided that she looked perfectly honest, so surely access to Kristin's apartment was in order? Especially as Chiew needed to take off early to visit her boyfriend in prison.

As soon as the maid left, Madison called Jake in the car and he came right up from the underground garage. The first thing they did was play back Kristin's answering machine. Right away they hit pay dirt: the second recorded message was from Mister X, requesting that Kristin meet him at the end of Santa Monica Pier on Sunday night.

"Let's go," Jake said.

"Where?" Madison said. "If she *did* meet him, it's highly unlikely they're still there."

"Maybe somebody saw them together."

"Then we need a picture of her. Did you take any?"

"No, but there's one of her with her sister in a frame in the living room."

"Get it," Madison said, still in her bossy mode, but

now just as anxious as Jake to find out what had happened to Kristin. She kept on hoping they wouldn't turn on the TV and hear about another body washed up on the beach.

While he was getting the photo, she took a quick look around. Nothing unusual. No clues. No jotted-down notes that might tell them more.

Jake brought her the photo. Kristin was indeed a dazzler—Madison had gotten a brief glimpse of her when she'd stopped by Jimmy Sica's to meet Jake for their date, but she'd honestly not appreciated how gorgeous the girl was. Fresh and natural with cascades of golden hair and a glowing smile. Nobody in their wildest dreams would tag her as a call girl.

"Whadda we do now?" Jake asked.

"Call Darlene," Madison said. "Let's see what it'll take to get her to cooperate."

chapter 25

*H*E'S NOT COMING BACK AND
there is no way I can escape from this room where I'm
being held a prisoner.

The words ran through Kristin's head as she lay
on the mattress in the small space, which was
now like an oven. She was trying to reserve her
strength.

*I'm tired, hungry, thirsty, hot, dispirited, ex-
hausted. And yet, I'm still alive. And so is Cherie. For
her sake I have to get out.*

But if he doesn't come back . . .

If he's left me to rot . . .

How long could a person last without food or
water? Was it days, weeks, months? How long?

She wanted to scream and cry out. Yell for
help.

But no. She couldn't do that. Had to stay strong for when HE came.

Mister X.

And he *would* come.

She knew he would.

chapter 26

"**B**YE, HONEY DOLL."

"Goodbye, Howard."

"Take good care of the ring."

"Of course."

"Give me two days an' I'll be there all ready to fuck your brains out."

"Such a romantic," Inga said with a superior smile. The only one getting fucked in this relationship was Howie. She'd put her true fiancé on hold while she collected as much jewelry as possible in as short a time as possible. Then she'd have the marriage annulled. Howie was an obvious playboy—she was merely getting revenge for all the women he'd used and abused.

Howie made an attempt to kiss his new wife on the lips. She not so gently shoved him away. "Please,

Howard, not in public," she scolded. "People are always watching me."

He lifted up her hand where the ten-carat diamond ring sparkled. Ten carats of cubic zirconia. When they'd been married a year and she presented him with a child, he'd buy her the real thing. People thought he was Howie Powers, schmucko playboy. They were wrong. There was much more to Howie than that.

He left the airport and drove back to town. The traffic was deadly, but Howie didn't care, he had the rest of the day all planned out.

Freddie Leon headed for Malibu, cursing the heavy traffic. He'd dropped Diana home first. There was something going on with her; she wasn't acting like herself. And what was this sudden attachment she had toward Max?

Maybe he should consider giving her more attention. He always put business first and she knew it.

And when he wanted to relax . . . well, it wasn't Diana he turned to. No. There was somebody else.

And today he desperately needed to relax.

Olive Deacon clutched Tucci's hand. "I killed him!" she wailed. "He's dead because of me!"

Her alcohol-drenched breath caused him to take a step back. "Who?" he asked.

"My husband, that's who!" she sobbed.

"Mrs. Deacon, I'm going to read you your rights. Anything you say may be used in evidence against you. You have the right to a lawyer. If—"

As he droned on she disintegrated before his very eyes. Her face crumpled, mascara coursed down her cheeks, lipstick stained her teeth.

"Mrs. Deacon," he said quietly, feeling sorry for her. "Do you want to contact your lawyer before we talk?"

"No lawyer," she said between sobs. "It's my fault Bo's dead. I've been punished, and I have to tell you everything."

"You wish to make a formal statement?"

"Yes, I do."

"Very well."

And before he could get his pen out, she began talking.

chapter 27

THE MOMENT SHE HEARD THE
click of the lock, Kristin was ready. She raced to the
door, positioning herself behind it, so that when he
opened it, there would be an element of surprise. Her
heart was pounding, but she knew that if she didn't
seize the opportunity all would be lost.

She was filled with anger as she crouched in position. Anger would make her strong. Anger would help
her gain her freedom.

Mister X pushed open the door.

She braced herself, holding the bed leg poised
above her head—ready to smash him with it—ready
to run.

Light flooded the dusty little room. He stepped
inside.

For a moment she was paralyzed, unable to move or
think. And then, as if in slow motion, she sprang

forward, sideswiping the figure in black with all her might—hitting him as hard as she could with the wooden bed leg.

To her amazement he didn't fall. In movies when you saw someone get hit they always fell. Instead he staggered, letting out a furious cry of surprise.

Before he had a chance to react further, she bashed him again.

This time he almost went down. His baseball cap fell to the ground, and his sunglasses hit the floor and cracked. Seizing her opportunity, she ran past him, through the door, out into the unknown, frantically trying to figure out the best way to freedom.

She found herself on a narrow, overgrown path. To her left, hundreds of feet below, was the ocean. Ahead of her there were steps hewn into the rock leading up to a big house perched high above.

The steps were her only way out. She raced toward them, concentrating on survival, not looking back.

As she reached the first step she could hear him behind her. He grabbed her leg. She kicked out blindly.

"Bitch!" he snarled.

"Leave me alone, you sick bastard!" she screamed, scrambling desperately up the hazardous steps.

He grabbed her again, this time getting hold of her makeshift dress. The sheet tore. Half naked, she continued to claw her way up, determined that he was not going to stop her. Nobody was. She was heading for freedom in every way—not just from this man, but this life.

"Don't you get it?" he yelled. "I own you. I always

have. You're *my* whore. My very own personal whore."

There was something about his voice . . . something she almost recognized. It wasn't the Mister X voice, the disguised growl. This was the real man talking, and it was . . . Oh God, SHE KNEW WHO HE WAS!

For a moment she could barely breathe. Then, as if in a trance, she stopped climbing and turned around.

The monster was two steps behind her, baseball cap gone along with the dark glasses. A trickle of blood rolled slowly down the side of his face.

She stared into his eyes.

He knew she recognized him.

They were both still, like two big cats in the wild, watching each other, waiting to see who would pounce first.

"Okay," he said at last. "So now you know. And there's *nothing* you can do." And he laughed, that self-loving cackle she remembered so well. "You and your dumb sister—you're exactly alike," he continued. "She was a whore, too. She didn't deserve to live. Neither do you."

In perfect slow motion she rose from her defensive position, brought her leg back and kicked out with such force that when her leg connected with his chest he had no chance to correct his balance.

He fell back, his hands clutching the air as he tumbled over himself twice, and then disappeared over the edge of the cliff with a long, bloodcurdling scream.

Kristin watched him fall, heard the sound of his

JACKIE COLLINS

body as it struck a tree on its way to the rocks and ocean below.

She wasn't sorry. She had finally avenged her sister. And it felt completely satisfying, as if it was meant to be.

Howie Powers would *never* laugh at anyone again.

Epilogue

Nine Months Later

DETECTIVE TUCCI AGITAT-
edly paced the corridors of Cedars Sinai. Faye was
giving birth and although he'd tried to stay in the
room holding her hand, the sight of blood—his wife's
blood—had sent him running.

His new partner, Wanda O'Donahue, had stopped
by to keep him company. She'd also brought a box of
donuts and a flask of Starbucks coffee. There were
many advantages to having a female partner, although Faye didn't seem to think so.

"How's it going in the delivery room?" Wanda
asked, biting into a donut.

"It's a war zone," he said, grimacing. "A lot of
blood and guts and screaming."

"You'll live," Wanda said, giving him a friendly pat
on the back.

Yeah, he'd live.

It had been some year. The murder of Salli T. Turner had garnered the most headlines, especially when Mrs. Bo Deacon had confessed, right after the terrible car accident which killed her husband.

Tucci had not felt that her confession rang true—although his superiors were in "we've caught the murderer" heaven, and the press went into headline overdrive. Olive simply didn't have the details the killer would have possessed, although she *was* able to produce the gun used to kill Froo. It was registered to Bo Deacon.

Tucci stayed on the case, establishing that Bobby Skorch had gone to his house earlier in the evening, made love to his wife, fought with her, and left, forever feeling guilty that he hadn't stayed around.

Bo Deacon had then arrived, unaware that Olive was following him. He'd come on to Salli, she'd told him he had no chance with her. A fight had ensued and he'd killed her in a frenzy of frustration. Then he'd shot the houseman and fled. Olive had observed everything from her hiding place in the bushes next to the pool.

When Olive had killed Bo in the car wreck, she'd been so overcome with guilt that she'd decided to take the blame for the murders and protect her husband's not-so-spotless reputation. At least in death, he would be her hero.

If it wasn't for Tucci and his concern for detail, she would have been incarcerated for life. As it was, she was soon back in her Bel Air mansion with a twenty-five-year-old boyfriend, a lucrative book deal, and a new passion for life.

Tucci took a swig of coffee. It tasted fine. For the

last six months he'd taken up spinning—an exhausting form of aerobic exercise on a stationary bike. It worked for him, and it had meant no more dieting, since he'd lost twenty-five pounds.

Faye's doctor approached him, a gentle Asian woman with the most captivating smile. "Your wife would like to see you now, Detective."

"Is it over?"

"Yes, it is."

"And?"

"You're the proud father of a beautiful baby girl."

His grin practically lit up the entire hospital.

The Freddie Leon divorce was one of the most expensive L.A. divorces in recent years. Diana received half of everything—and everything was a lot. Freddie decided it was worth it. He had his freedom and no price was too high to obtain *that*. Besides, business was fine; he could afford to pay Diana off.

A discreet six months after the final decree, Ria Santiago moved into Freddie's beach house—he'd given the Bel Air mausoleum to Diana. After a seven-year affair, he and Ria were finally able to be seen together in public. Freddie felt it was the least he could do for the most loyal woman he'd ever met.

Out of the hospital and fitter than ever, Max Steele eschewed a lot of his material possessions. He traded in his Maserati for a Hummer. Sold his house and moved into the Wilshire high-rise he'd been leasing out. Did not replace his gold Rolex, and after trying to contact Kristin a couple of times and getting no response, he'd fallen in lust with Angela Musconni, even though it was against policy since the agency represented her. Of course, he'd had to persuade Angie to dump the loser she was living with, but that hadn't been too difficult, since shortly after they got together, Eddie Stoner scored a TV series that shot in Hawaii.

It was amazing what could be accomplished when you were one of the most powerful agents in town.

Blaming himself for Salli's death, Bobby Skorch lost all sense of concentration. While attempting a record-breaking motorcycle jump between skyscrapers in New York, he faltered and fell to his death.

Natalie De Barge got the anchor job she'd been yearning for. Sitting beside Jimmy Sica every night, they made a fine couple. When the cameras weren't rolling, she practically had to beat him off with a stick, but that was just one of the hazards of being an anchorwoman.

She put her love life on hold and enjoyed every second of her new invigorating career.

Her brother, Cole, moved in with Mister Mogul—who so far was treating him like a prince. However, to Natalie's eternal relief, Cole was smart enough not to give up his day job.

Junia took the twenty thousand dollars she received for revealing all of Darlene's dark secrets, and moved to Nashville, where she met a blond and bubbly country singing star with enormous breasts. They soon became a couple. Junia took up singing. She wasn't half bad.

* * *

Darlene was finally nailed on that good old stand-by—tax evasion. Her lawyer, Linden Masters, was so livid to discover she'd kept things from him that he refused to represent her anymore. She hired a new lawyer with even more savvy than Linden, and because of her powerful connections, she got off with an extremely short jail term.

After she got out, she threw all caution out the window and found a ghostwriter to collaborate on a book, naming names. Her book—dramatically entitled *Madam*—was due out shortly.

Hollywood waited in a state of paranoid fascination.

Kristin took stock of her life, and her sister's too. She met with Cherie's doctor and finally listened to exactly what he had to say. He was a nice man with brown hair and kindly eyes. "There are no miracles, Kristin," he informed her. "Cherie is brain-dead. The only reason she's still alive is because you won't allow us to pull the plug."

"Pull it," she said quietly. "I understand."

"You're sure?"

"Yes, I'm sure."

After escaping from the beach house, she'd come home and anonymously called the police—telling them all she knew about Mister X, including his death and where they'd find him.

Jake had been frantic to see her, so she had agreed to have lunch with him and to listen to everything he had to say. It wasn't enough though—there was no going back. He was part of her past now, and she was moving forward.

He told her about the story his friend Madison Castelli was working on.

"Do me this one favor, Jake, leave my name out of it."

"It's done," he assured her.

A week later she moved out of her luxurious apartment into a simpler place.

A few weeks later the doctor called and invited her to dinner. "What are you going to do now that you no longer have to pay your sister's bills?" he asked.

"I'm going back to school," she said. "I want to get my degree in child psychology and maybe—sometime in the future—work with children."

"Sounds like an excellent idea."

The doctor didn't lead a glamorous life or drive a flashy car. He was a hardworking professional who really cared for people, and he genuinely liked her for herself. Kristin found a great deal of comfort in his presence. So much so that they were married three months later.

Jake Sica stayed in L.A. for several months, photographing movie and sports stars, singers and moguls. Working for *Manhattan Style* was an interesting gig, and very highly paid, but after a while he began to yearn for the wide-open spaces of Arizona.

One morning he woke up, looked out his window at the hovering smog, and decided that was it.

By noon he was packed and on his way.

Madison wrote the best story of her career, all about the call-girl business in Hollywood. It was so good that Hollywood shelled out, bought the movie rights for an astronomical sum, and asked her to work on the script.

She stayed in touch with her good friend Jake. He was a great guy, but they never quite connected romantically. Wrong timing.

She took a weekend off with her parents in Connecticut. They were delighted to see her, especially her handsome father, Michael.

Then she flew to Hollywood and met Alex Woods, an edgy, incredibly talented writer/producer/director with a penchant for making powerful Oscar-nominated movies. He wanted to make *her* movie.

So Madison entered the next phase of her life with her eyes open and an appetite for excitement.

Things were looking up.

Jackie Collins

America's Most Sensational Novelist

Jackie Collins knows what really goes on inside Hollywood — the affairs, the double-dealing, the passions, the drama. She burst into the limelight with her best-selling novel HOLLYWOOD WIVES. Read it and her other novels — Jackie Collins exposes the glamorous world of the stars in every book.

- ☐ AMERICAN STAR 02349-7/$7.99
- ☐ LADY BOSS 02347-0/$7.99
- ☐ HOLLYWOOD WIVES 70459-1/$6.99
- ☐ LUCKY 02348-9/$7.99
- ☐ HOLLYWOOD HUSBANDS 72451-7/$6.99
- ☐ ROCK STAR 70880-5/$6.99
- ☐ HOLLYWOOD KIDS 89849-3/$6.99
- ☐ THRILL! 02094-3/$7.99
- ☐ POWER 02458-2/$3.99
- ☐ OBSESSION 02459-0/$3.99

AVAILABLE FROM POCKET BOOKS

POCKET
BOOKS